PUFFIN BOOKS

# DEAD BALL

Tom Palmer is a football fan and author. He writes two series for Puffin: Football Academy and Foul Play. He visits schools and libraries every week to talk about reading, writing and football.

It was reading about football that helped Tom to become a confident reader. He now has the job of his dreams: travelling the world to watch football matches, meeting players, then writing stories about them.

He lives in Yorkshire, where he likes to be with his family, watch football and eat Dubble chocolate bars.

You can find out more about Tom – and talk to him – through his website *www.tompalmer.co.uk*

*Books by Tom Palmer*

*Foul Play series (in reading order)*

FOUL PLAY

DEAD BALL

OFF SIDE

*For younger readers*

*Football Academy series (in reading order)*

BOYS UNITED

STRIKING OUT

THE REAL THING

READING THE GAME

FREE KICK

CAPTAIN FANTASTIC

THE SECRET FOOTBALL CLUB

# DEAD BALL

## TOM PALMER

PUFFIN

PUFFIN BOOKS

Published by the Penguin Group
Penguin Books Ltd, 80 Strand, London WC2R 0RL, England
Penguin Group (USA) Inc., 375 Hudson Street, New York, New York 10014, USA
Penguin Group (Canada), 90 Eglinton Avenue East, Suite 700, Toronto, Ontario, Canada M4P 2Y3
(a division of Pearson Penguin Canada Inc.)
Penguin Ireland, 25 St Stephen's Green, Dublin 2, Ireland (a division of Penguin Books Ltd)
Penguin Group (Australia), 250 Camberwell Road, Camberwell, Victoria 3124, Australia
(a division of Pearson Australia Group Pty Ltd)
Penguin Books India Pvt Ltd, 11 Community Centre, Panchsheel Park, New Delhi – 110 017, India
Penguin Group (NZ), 67 Apollo Drive, Rosedale, North Shore 0632, New Zealand
(a division of Pearson New Zealand Ltd)
Penguin Books (South Africa) (Pty) Ltd, 24 Sturdee Avenue, Rosebank,
Johannesburg 2196, South Africa

Penguin Books Ltd, Registered Offices: 80 Strand, London WC2R 0RL, England

puffinbooks.com

First published 2009, reissued 2010
008



Set in Sabon 12.5/17.25pt
Typeset by Palimpsest Book Production Limited, Grangemouth, Stirlingshire
Made and printed in England by Clays Ltd, St Ives plc



British Library Cataloguing in Publication Data
A CIP catalogue record for this book is available from the British Library

ISBN: 978-0-141-32368-8

www.greenpenguin.co.uk

Penguin Books is committed to a sustainable future for our business, our readers and our planet. This book is made from Forest Stewardship Council™ certified paper.

*For Rebecca and Iris*

Reviews from some of Tom's fans for

# Foul Play

'It was a truly brilliant book. When I grow up I want to be a football author' – **Charlie**

'I am an eleven-year-old and I have read your book. I love it and hope *Dead Ball* will be released soon' – **Ravi**

'I have read *Foul Play*. I think it is really good. It has a lot of adventure in it' – **Susan**

'Really, really, really good. Clever, well written. Very good for people like me who like football' – **Daniel**

'I like it – it's my best book' – **Samuel**

'I think this book is so good I read it three times'– **Yusupha**

'Perfect. Best story I have ever read' – **Mohammed**

'I like the way the story is full, instead of stopping to put in boring effects' – **Ryan**

# CONTENTS

# WEDNESDAY

## *WORLD CUP QUALIFIER*

'Come on, England!' Danny shouted at the television.

On the screen England's star striker, Sam Roberts, collected the ball up in the centre circle. He played it wide to the national team's short but speedy winger. The winger moved slowly at first, then accelerated past two Russian defenders and played an early ball into the box. Roberts was already bearing down on the penalty area, having run half the length of the pitch in seconds.

He leapt for the ball.

'Go on!' Danny was on the edge of his seat now. Literally. Ready to leap in the air if Roberts scored.

Roberts met the ball with his head. Full on.

But Danny's sister, Emily, was on her feet now. 'Ha ha,' she shouted. 'What a donkey.'

Roberts' header had gone wide. Well wide.

Emily turned to face the rest of the room: her brother, his friend Paul, her mum and dad.

'Come on, *Russia*!' she shouted.

'He missed,' Danny said, turning to his dad. Danny did this automatically whenever they were at the football or just watching it on TV. His dad was blind. And Danny was his commentator.

'I gathered,' Dad said. Then in a very different voice: 'Sit down, Emily.'

Dad knew that Emily was really getting to Danny now. Throughout the game she'd been trying to wind her brother up, saying she wanted Russia to win, not England. Cheering when Russia did well; mocking Danny when England messed up.

'Yes, Emily,' Mum said. 'Either sit down or go and do something else. You hate football. You're only doing this to annoy your brother.'

Danny said nothing. He couldn't even look at his sister. He was absolutely furious. It was worse than sitting with a *real* fan of another team. At least then you knew they felt as much about their team as you did about yours.

'Why should I?' Emily said. 'I support Russia.'

Danny knew it was best to leave his sister to it. If he reacted angrily to her she'd have won. And today she was being particularly unpleasant. Having been dumped by her boyfriend. Two hours ago. By text.

Danny smiled.

But not for long.

Because *Russia* were attacking now. Their keeper had flung the ball half the length of the pitch and suddenly their giant blond forward was bearing down on goal. The England defenders couldn't get near him. The forward went past a first and a second, then played a one-two with his striking partner. And *bang*: a shot on goal from fifteen yards. Only Alex Finn, the England keeper, to beat. The ball flew straight and hard. Impossible to reach.

Emily was on her feet again. 'YeaaaaAAAAHHH.'

Danny looked away from her in disgust. He kept his attention on the screen, to see Alex Finn dive low, stretching his arm out as far as he could. And – impossibly – tipping the ball round the post.

'What a save!' Danny said, standing up himself now. 'What a fantastic save! You should have seen it, Dad. He should never have got to it.'

Then he stared at his sister, who'd sat down scowling.

The commentator agreed with Danny: '*The City and England keeper is playing as if his life depended on it!*'

Moments later the ref's whistle blew. Half-time. England 0 Russia 0.

But a draw wasn't good enough: England needed to *win* this game. It was a World Cup qualifier. Everybody agreed that you had to win your home games to have a chance of qualifying for the finals.

'We're still going to win,' Emily declared. 'Then your precious England – and your even more precious Sam Roberts – won't go to the World Cup.'

'We?' Mum said to Emily. 'Since when were *you* Russian?'

Paul, who had said nothing up to this point, looked at Danny's sister and said, '*Vlady vorksvet*?'

Emily stared at him. 'What's that supposed to mean?'

'It's Russian,' Paul said.

Danny grinned at his friend. 'Don't you understand? Being a Russia fan?' he said.

Emily narrowed her eyes and stared at her brother. But she had nothing more to say.

The second half of the game was more open. End to end stuff. England and Russia equally matched.

There were two key points in the half that decided the result.

The first was a Russian attack, catching England on the break. Four attackers against two defenders.

The Russians moved so quickly there was nothing the defenders could do. Suddenly it was two strikers against Alex Finn. Again. The first striker lobbed Finn, but somehow Finn leapt and tipped the ball on to the bar. But, instead of going out for a corner, the ball bounced back into play, to the other Russian striker. The second striker took his time. He controlled the ball, then side-footed it past Finn.

'GooooaaaAAALLL,' shouted Emily, on her feet again.

Except the ball *hadn't* gone past Finn. And it *wasn't* a goal. As he was recovering from the lob, the England keeper managed to stick his foot out and deflect the ball wide for a corner.

A miraculous save.

Danny turned to smile at Emily.

His sister had the same look on her face as the Russian forwards. Disbelief.

'Sit down, Emily,' Danny's dad said quietly.

Then, with just one minute to go, England attacked for what had to be the last time.

The ball was played wide to the speedy winger again. He had no time for fancy tricks. He had to get the ball into the penalty area. As soon as possible. So, without hesitating, he sent over a long and deep cross.

At first it looked like nobody could possibly reach it. But Sam Roberts was running. From the centre circle. Like an express train. So fast it seemed that everybody else had stopped to watch. Suddenly he was in the penalty area, with the ball flying towards the far post.

Roberts lunged at the ball. His leg stretched out as far as a leg can stretch.

His boot hit the ball.

The ball hit the back of the net.

And Danny and Paul stood, arms aloft, right in front of Emily, but saying nothing.

Emily folded her arms, crossed her legs and stared fiercely at the screen.

And, because of the wild celebrations in the stadium

and in front rooms and pubs across England, few noticed Sam Roberts lying in agony, his leg bent in a way legs aren't meant to bend, blood seeping through his white England sock.

## *MATCH FIXERS*

The mobile rang seconds after the final whistle.

A man in his sixties stiffened. He was English. Sitting on the deck of his luxury yacht in St Katharine's Dock, London.

The man used to be known by another name. A name well known in sporting circles. But, to the people who worked for him now, he was Kenneth Francis, a millionaire who had made his money in banking.

Francis had no option but to pick up. He knew who it was at the end of the line.

'What shall we be doing with Alex Finn?' a voice said. A Russian voice. There was no time for pleasantries. No *hello, how are you, how's the family*.

'Good evening, Dmitri,' the Englishman said.

'It is *not* a good evening. It is a *bad* evening.'

'Yes,' Francis said. 'A bad evening indeed.'

He wasn't quite sure how best to deal with this phone call. Because the man on the other end of the phone – Dmitri Tupolev – was one of the richest men in the world. He had more money than the Queen. Billions. More sports cars than you'd see at an F1 Grand Prix. And more planes than you could fit on a runway. He had made his money in Russia. Out of oil, gas, corruption. And murder.

Kenneth Francis gazed out of his yacht. The lights from nearby buildings reflected off the water. It was here – at this dock – that he had first met Dmitri Tupolev, when the Russian's enormous yacht had eased in alongside his. The Englishman's yacht *had* been the biggest in the dock. Until then.

'I repeat. What shall we be doing with the England goalkeeper?' Tupolev said. 'He has disappointed me.'

'Me too, Dmitri. Me too,' Francis replied. 'But we must be careful.'

'My friend,' Tupolev said. 'Your Alex Finn may have cost my country a position in the World Cup Finals. I expect you to have spoken to him. Told him that it will be clever of him to let Russia score the goals.'

'I did, Dmitri. I did. And Finn let us down. But I think we need to be careful. Not to do something rash that would upset the rest of our plans.'

Francis chose his words carefully. He needed to stay on good terms with Dmitri Tupolev. Because the Russian billionaire was the key to his future. Because together they were planning to make a bid to buy one of the world's most famous football clubs. But first – out of goodwill – Francis had agreed to help Tupolev to fix two matches. World Cup qualifiers between England and Russia. And to fix them both in favour of the Russians.

Francis hoped that, in return, Tupolev would be happy to part with somewhere in the region of £400 million to help him buy City FC. A club that had just come on the market. Francis wanted control of City more than anything. And if it meant England failing to qualify for another tournament, then so what?

Although he was rich, the Englishman was not rich enough to lay his hands on a spare £400 million. He had about half that amount stashed away. In Swiss accounts. Under several names. He used to have more. Including properties and cars *and* a football club of his own. But he'd lost it all.

Kenneth Francis realized that he was not coming across well in the telephone conversation. He needed to appear more decisive. Utterly decisive, in fact. England v Russia was the first game between the two teams. But they had to play each other again. In Russia. *Next* Wednesday. If Russia won that, then they would be back at the top of Group F. And Tupolev would probably be happy.

Francis knew that he had to keep Tupolev happy anyway. Tupolev was a man who was alleged to be responsible for at least thirty murders. Of journalists, sportspeople, politicians and business rivals. Even former girlfriends. He was not a man to be messed with.

'Dmitri?'

'Yes, my friend?'

There was something menacing about the way Tupolev said *my friend*. It was almost as if he meant *quite* the opposite.

'Dmitri. I will deal with it. Tomorrow Alex Finn will have an accident. Then I will contact his England understudy, Matt McGee. He will be quite clear why Finn had his accident. Russia will win the return match. Have no fear. Tell me what score you would like it to be.'

# *THURSDAY*

## *WORK EXPERIENCE*

Danny got off the bus in the centre of town and walked the length of Wellington Street to the newspaper offices.

The city centre was not how he knew it. When he came into town at the weekend – with his dad or to meet his friends – it was full of younger people and children. As well as adults. But today it was adults only. All dressed in black. All walking quickly. All looking miserable.

It was the fourth day of Danny's work experience. The year-tens were out of school for a fortnight. Danny's friend Paul was working in a computer software office – mending joysticks. Charlotte was sorting files at police HQ. Other friends were sweeping hair off the floor, putting books out on shelves, distributing staples at a TV station. And one was painting a perimeter fence at an undertaker's. Black.

But Danny was working at the regional newspaper, the *Evening Post*. Assisting the Chief Sportswriter.

Once he'd got through reception, Danny sprinted up three flights of stairs. He was eager to know what the Chief Sportswriter thought of the match the night before. He'd have written his report on the way back from Wembley Stadium first thing this morning. On the train from King's Cross.

Danny reached the top of the stairs. He went along a corridor, taking the third door on the left. He passed three desks – two journalists said hello – and knocked on a hollow wooden door at the end of the large office.

'Come in, Danny.'

Danny opened the door and closed it quietly behind him.

Anton Holt was at his desk, frowning at his laptop screen. He held his hand up, then pointed at a pile of newspapers. That meant he was in the middle of writing, still finishing his match report, maybe; and that Danny should have a seat and read the day's papers.

So Danny started work, smiling. There were all the day's papers, plus *FourFourTwo*, *World Soccer* and *Match of the Day* magazines.

Work?

Reading about football was about as good as *work* could get.

The reason Danny had got such a good work placement was because he knew Anton Holt.

They'd met four months before. First at a City press conference. Then in a hail of bullets at the football stadium.

It had started when Danny witnessed the kidnap of

England's leading scorer, Sam Roberts. City's chairman, Sir Richard Gawthorpe, claimed a terrorist group had kidnapped Roberts. Danny and Holt had solved the mystery and rescued the player. They had been in touch ever since.

Sir Richard, the real kidnapper, however, had disappeared, despite a Europe-wide hunt. Most people assumed he was dead.

Danny read several headlines in that morning's papers.

**ALEX FINN-ISHES RUSSIANS**
**ALEXANDER THE GREAT**
**THE RUSSIANS ARE ~~COMING~~ GOING**

Alex Finn had been awarded nine out of ten in some papers.

But the big news for Danny was Sam Roberts. A broken shin, shattered against the goalpost after he'd scored the winner. Danny looked at the photo: Roberts being carried off on a stretcher, his face twisted in agony. But still raising his arm to wave at the crowd, eighty thousand people standing to applaud him.

'He'll be out for months,' Anton Holt said, shutting the lid of his laptop.

'How bad is it?' Danny asked.

'A clean break. He'll be three months in a pot. Then

three – at least three – building his leg up again. Then his fitness. He'll miss most of the season.'

Danny put his head in his hands. This was terrible. Roberts wasn't only England's leading scorer. He was City's. Without him, their chances of a decent run in the Champions' League were poor.

'Good game, though,' Holt said.

'Yeah.' Danny nodded. That moment when he turned to stare at his sister after Roberts had scored would stay with him for a long time.

'Anyway,' Holt said, 'to work.'

'What can I do?'

'Join me. Down the pub.'

Danny frowned.

'Three o'clock this afternoon,' Holt smiled. 'You, me and the newspaper's editor, a nice country pub, interviewing . . . Alex Finn. He's giving us an exclusive interview about his performance last night.'

Danny grinned. He couldn't believe how lucky he was.

'How did you manage that?' he said to Holt.

'It wasn't me,' Holt said, looking sheepish. 'The editor of the paper is in the same golf club as Finn's dad. That's how.'

After Danny had phoned his dad to check it was OK to be home late, he got to work. If he was going to meet Alex Finn he wanted to know as much about him as he could.

He typed 'Alex Finn' into the Internet browser on Holt's laptop, while the journalist was busy elsewhere.

This was the sort of thing Danny did in his spare time anyway. At home Danny's bedroom was not so much a bedroom, but an office. A private detective's office. He had a desk, a swivel chair – and a huge map of his city on the wall.

From his office he would track crimes. He'd scour the local paper, following them from their first reports in the news section to the court cases. He even went to watch the court cases sometimes. Gathering information to see if he could work out the clues to solve the crimes.

He read the results on Alex Finn:

**Alex Finn** keeps England World Cup hopes alive

The England keeper, **Alex Finn** . . . series of saves against Russia . . . frustrated Russians . . . one of the great goalkeeping performances in an England shirt in modern times . . .

**www.soccerdaily.co.uk**

**Finn** signs for City

**Alex Finn**, United's long-time keeper, has switched to City . . . twelve-million-pound deal . . . three-year contract . . . 'I am thrilled to be at City. I've supported them since I was a . . .'

**www.footballnews.co.uk**

**Alex Finn**-ishes books

**Alex Finn** launched a literacy programme, helping boys to enjoy reading . . . about football. His favourite book is a novel called *Keeper* by Mal Peet . . .

**www.literacyengland.org.uk**

McGee in counterfeit scandal

Understudy to England keeper **Alex Finn**, Matt McGee was fined £500 for handling counterfeit money at City Court on 20 August. Found to be handling the money, he refused to say . . . . Although McGee is not thought to be a counterfeiter himself, he is alleged to have connections with organized crime . . . He was defended by his sister, Ruth McGee, the famous ballet dancer . . .

**www.footballtittletattle.com**

Danny was transfixed.

It was very interesting that Finn enjoyed books. Danny thought he'd ask him about what books he'd read, whether he liked crime books.

Danny was into crime books as well as crime. Well

into them. That was why he'd got involved in the Sam Roberts kidnap. And that was why he wanted to be a detective.

Danny had read crime stories to his dad and had since become obsessed with crime. And, although he was enjoying the work experience at the newspaper, pretending that he was a journalist, what he really wanted to be was a detective. He wanted to know about crimes, find out all the details, then solve them. Like he had with Sam Roberts.

Reading up on Alex Finn to help with the interview was a bit like finding out details about a crime, so he could be better informed to solve it. The more facts he had for either job, the better prepared he'd be.

But Danny knew that Matt McGee was a much more interesting character than Alex Finn. All the stuff about McGee and the counterfeit money was no surprise. In fact, Danny had known there was something different about McGee since the moment he'd seen him. A few weeks ago.

Danny had been watching a trial at the courts. A well-known criminal from a neighbouring town was on trial for being involved in selling drugs. Gavin Barnes. He'd got off like he always did, because no one would ever dare to testify against him. But, during the lunch break of the trial, Danny had gone for a sandwich in a small park quite a way from the court house. Just to clear his mind. And there – to his disbelief – he'd seen the criminal who was on trial. *With* Matt McGee. Talking. Laughing. Then shaking hands.

Danny had done nothing with the information. It meant nothing. Not yet.

# LUNCH BREAK

Danny was nervous going into the café. It was full of adults. White shirts. Black jackets slung over the backs of their chairs. Three people tapping away on laptops. Others talking about their lives in loud voices. All with a background soundtrack of jazz music.

Danny wished he was somewhere else. He hated jazz music.

But he changed his mind when he saw who he'd come to meet. Her hair was a bit longer now, falling down to her shoulders.

Charlotte Duncan. Her mouth wrapped round a panini.

Danny got himself a sandwich and a cup of tea. He liked coffee too. But listening to all the people in the queue asking for decaf skinny lattes with extra shots of blah-blah-blah made him want to ask for tea. No fuss. Just a mug of tea.

He was pleased Charlotte had bagged a corner table. Somewhere relatively quiet. And comfy seats too. He put his tea and sandwich down and perched on the seat opposite her. His heart was beating fast. He could feel his face going pink.

'How's it going at the paper?' Charlotte asked, smiling.

Danny grimaced.

'What?' Charlotte said, bemused.

'This is just weird, isn't it?' he said. 'Like we've got jobs or something.'

'But we have.'

'Yeah, but it's still weird.'

That was what had been bothering Danny coming in here. Why he was feeling so uncomfortable. It wasn't the jazz music or the white shirts or the hundred kinds of coffee. It was that they were here on their lunch break. Like they really worked in the centre of town.

'So how is it?' Charlotte said, still with a puzzled look on her face.

'What?'

'The paper. You and Anton what's-his-name?'

'Great.' Danny leaned forward. 'And guess what?'

'What?'

'We're only going to interview *Alex Finn* this afternoon. In a pub in the countryside!'

Charlotte nodded.

'Who's Alex Finn?' she said.

Danny and Charlotte went to the same school. Four months ago they had become friends. Around the time the Sam Roberts stuff was going on. Danny had wanted them to be more than friends, but so far nothing had happened.

They'd been to the cinema. They hung out with a group of friends after school sometimes. But that was it. In fact, they'd seen *less* of each other recently.

But Danny had asked to meet her today for a reason. A good reason. Charlotte's work experience was with the police and Danny wanted to know what it was like. At least, that's what he told himself.

'So,' he asked casually, 'what have they had you doing today? The police, I mean.'

Charlotte looked at each of the tables around them, then turned to Danny and lowered her voice. 'We've been doing surveillance,' she said.

Danny's eyes widened. 'What? Who?'

'There's a criminal gang operating out of the market in town. We're watching them from a tower block. They're expecting a delivery today.' Charlotte looked around again. 'Class A drugs,' she whispered.

Danny was spellbound, watching Charlotte's mouth.

Now he felt envy. Pure envy. Would he rather be meeting international footballers with Anton Holt or observing major drug deals with Charlotte Duncan?

Both.

He wanted both.

He saw Charlotte's mouth open out into a smile. And then she was laughing. Loudly.

'What?' Danny said.

He noticed men looking over and he blushed again.

'You believed me,' Charlotte said. 'You think they'd have me doing that? You're such a mug. They've had me putting stuff on to computers.'

Danny frowned.

'Inputting data.' Charlotte went on. 'Typing. It's about as exciting as one of Mr Hinchliffe's English lessons.'

Danny tried to look like he didn't care that Charlotte had called him a mug. If Paul had said it, he'd not have been bothered. But there was something different about Charlotte saying it.

'So you've not got anything for me?' he said in a hard voice.

'What?' Now it was Charlotte's turn to frown.

But Danny had to go on.

'Nothing about CID? Anything going on?'

'Nothing,' Charlotte said, looking away.

And Danny felt small. Really small. Maybe Charlotte thought he had only asked her for a coffee because he wanted to know about the police.

And the worst thing was – it was partly true.

'How's your mum and dad?' Danny said, trying to change the subject.

'Fine,' she said. 'And your mum and dad? How are *they*?'

She was taking the mick now. How could he get out of this situation? Be honest. That's what his dad always said. Be straightforward with people.

'I didn't just want to meet you to ask about the police,' Danny said. 'I like meeting you. And we haven't seen each other for a bit.'

Charlotte sat back in her chair. She smiled. 'Actually, I have read some interesting things in the stuff I'm inputting.'

'Yeah?' Danny tried to sound only slightly interested. But he leaned forward – ready to listen.

# APPOINTMENT WITH ALEX FINN

3 p.m. Danny sat outside the pub at a wooden table – that was on the edge of the car park and a lawn – while Anton Holt and his boss, Giles Forshaw, the newspaper's editor, went inside.

Danny was feeling deeply envious. All the way from the newspaper offices, Holt and Forshaw had talked only about their travelling to Moscow on Sunday. On the players' flight. He wished he could go. Imagine going to Russia to watch the football. With the team!

Danny stared across fields that sloped down to a river. Further up the river there was a ruin. An abbey. Danny remembered his dad bringing him here years ago. They used to come a lot. And eat here sometimes. When his dad still had his sight. He smiled at the memory.

But it didn't allay his nerves. His big worry was that Alex Finn would arrive before Holt and his boss came back. Then he'd have to talk to Finn. Alone.

What do you say to England's number one if he comes and sits on the seat next to you the night after he's played a blinder for his country? *Well played last night, Alex.* Something like that?

Danny smiled.

Until he saw a silver Mercedes move slowly into the car park. It crunched on the gravel as its driver edged it backwards into a parking space next to a Porsche.

Danny shivered. He had a thing about Mercedes cars. Ever since the madman and former football chairman Sir Richard Gawthorpe had tried to run him over in *his* Mercedes.

Danny watched as the driver got out.

It was Alex Finn, his pair of sunglasses not disguising him. He looked around the car park for a long time before he shut the door and moved away from his car. He appeared hesitant, like he was trying to avoid someone.

Danny was surprised to see how tall Finn was. He knew he was six-four. He had it on a trading card. But seeing him was different. He was huge. Massive shoulders. Long legs and arms. Like a statue of a man made bigger than a real man should be.

He practised his line: *Well played last night, Alex.* Or should he call him Mr Finn?

Finn walked towards Danny.

This was it.

'Alex? Over here.'

Danny watched as Finn turned towards Giles Forshaw by the door to the pub. He saw Finn wave, then head over to the newspaper's editor, who had been joined by Holt. The three men stood in a triangle.

Danny took in the scene: three men at a pub, surrounded by trees and posh cars, a hill sloping up behind them. After a few moments they came over to Danny, Holt carrying a tray of coffees and a Coke for Danny.

'And this is Danny,' Forshaw said. 'He's doing work experience with Anton. Just for a couple of weeks.'

Danny put out his hand. Finn shook it. The hand was enormous. Really enormous. Danny had wanted to be like one of the adults, but seeing his hand dwarfed by the keeper's, he felt even more like a child.

The three men sat down with Danny.

'First of all, Alex,' Forshaw said. 'You played a great game last night. Those saves – wonderful.'

'Thanks,' Finn said. His voice was quiet. Muted. He wasn't what Danny had expected. And Danny noticed he kept glancing at the car park entrance every time a car came by on the main road.

'We'd like to do a piece on how you feel about the World Cup campaign,' Forshaw went on. 'If you have dreams of being the first England keeper to have a decent chance of winning it since Gordon Banks, etc. What do you think?'

Finn smiled and raised his hand. 'I could dream it,' he said. 'But it's a bit early to be thinking that way. We need to qualify first. One game at a time and all that. Plus, I should say that I don't assume I'll be the first-choice keeper in eighteen months' time, when the tournament's on. There're two more great keepers in the squad. Skatie. And McGee.'

'McGee?' Forshaw said. 'He's never going to get a game ahead of you. And he's – well – not the best role model in the world.' As he said this Forshaw glanced at Danny.

There it was again. Someone else talking about Matt McGee, England's second- or third-choice keeper, like there was something bad about him. Danny was interested. Especially because the person was the editor of a major newspaper: if anyone should know stuff like that, he should. Danny wished he could ask questions. All these rumours. Was there any truth in them?

'Matt McGee's straight,' Finn said. 'And a good mate. If you don't mind, Giles, I'd rather we didn't add to the speculation.'

Danny noticed Giles Forshaw blush bright red as Anton Holt took over seamlessly.

'Tell us a bit about the game last night, Alex. What would you say was the key point of the match?'

The men talked about the game. In detail. But Danny's mind was whirring. Matt McGee. Professional footballer. Had a difficult youth. Involved in crime, possibly. He certainly spent time with criminals: Danny knew that. A gambler. Debts. Danny decided he would fill in a few pages about McGee. Back at his desk in his bedroom.

After they'd talked about the game, Anton turned to Danny and said, 'Have you got any questions, Danny?'

Danny's mind froze. *Say something intelligent. Quick!* he thought.

'Errrrm . . . Are you worried about the away game?' Danny said. 'In Russia, on Wednesday. They play on a synthetic surface. Do you think that'll be a disadvantage?'

Finn smiled at Danny. 'Good question,' he said. 'You'll have to watch this lad, Giles. One for the future?'

Forshaw nodded enthusiastically, glad that Finn wasn't cross with him for his question about McGee.

'I think it'll be harder,' Finn said to Danny. 'A lot harder. But the Luzhniki is a great stadium. I've played there with City.'

'Spartak away,' Danny said quickly. 'I remember. You kept a clean sheet.'

'That's right. Spot on. And the plastic pitch *was* difficult that night. But we've trained for it. We should be OK. And – like you say – I have good memories of the stadium. We got through to the semis there, didn't we?'

'Yes. To play Real,' Danny said.

'Did you go?' Finn asked Danny. 'I mean, have you been away in Europe?'

'No,' Danny replied. 'Not yet. Not to see City. But I've seen England. This year in the European Championships.'

'Yeah?' Finn said. 'That was pretty good. But I think it would have gone a lot better if there hadn't been all that terrible stuff with Sam. He wasn't right in the finals. But you can't blame *him*.'

Danny glanced at Holt and grinned.

'Yeah, you know all about that, Anton,' Finn said.

Holt nodded, smiling at Danny.

Even though Danny had saved Sam Roberts four months earlier, rescuing him from Sir Richard Gawthorpe and his cronies, people thought that Anton Holt and two painter-decorators had saved him. Danny's name had been kept out of the press; his parents had insisted. And Danny wasn't bothered anyway.

The interview continued. Danny listened, but asked no more questions. Nor Holt. Forshaw was leading the interview.

Danny cast his eyes across at the abbey again. He wished his dad was here. He'd have loved this. Sitting in one of his favourite places, enjoying the peace and quiet. It was silent, except for the odd fancy car pulling up in the car park. Porsches. Mercedes. A Rolls-Royce. All with personalized number plates.

And, most recently, a black Range Rover, tinted

windows, that arrived and parked up, at the far side of the car park where only Danny could see it.

Like he always did, Danny noted its number plate. Not personalized, he was pleased to see. He hated personalized number plates: what a waste of money! He also noted that no one got into it – or out of it.

Eventually Finn said he needed to go. Everyone stood.

'Any chance of a couple more questions?' Forshaw begged.

Finn looked at his watch. 'Come with me. In the Merc. I'll give you a lift into town. How's that?'

Giles Forshaw – a man in his fifties – grinned like a toddler.

And off they went. Forshaw and Finn. Into the Mercedes.

Unaware that unfriendly eyes were watching them.

## THE CRASH

'He's all right, isn't he?' Danny said to Holt.

'Finn? He is. A gent. Not one of those players who are up their own ...' Holt paused. 'You know ... It's hard to get an interview with a player these days. They'd rather walk past you, head down, than stop for a chat.'

They were driving behind Alex Finn's Mercedes along a country road, back towards town.

Danny grinned. 'So what's Matt McGee like?'

'Why do you ask that?' Holt said.

'It was what your boss said about him. And I saw something online this morning too. About his dodgy past.'

Holt frowned. 'McGee's an interesting character. He didn't come into football like most do these days. Through the academies, I mean. McGee was in a pub team from sixteen to twenty, then he got picked up by Leeds United, then he moved to City.'

'What's so dodgy about that?'

'Well ... some of his mates,' Holt said, slowing down as a black Range Rover overtook them. 'They were involved in ... criminal activity. Allegedly. And then there's the counterfeit stuff.'

Danny's ears pricked up. 'What sort of criminal activity?'

'Theft. Cars. Stuff like that.'

'Was it McGee?'

'There's no evidence . . .'

'But people like to speculate?' Danny suggested.

'That's right,' Holt said. 'And there's his gambling. He has gambling debts. Some say massive: like hundreds of thousands. But he's all right. All the times I've had anything to do with him, he's been OK. And Finn seemed to vouch for him . . .'

But Danny had stopped listening to Holt. He was watching the car in front of them. The black Range Rover that had just overtaken them. It was the one from the car park. Same number plate. Danny was sure.

'That Range Rover . . .' Danny said.

'What about it?'

'It was at the pub.'

'Another flash . . . person,' Holt said.

The Range Rover was tailgating Finn's Mercedes now. Too close, Danny thought. Something was wrong.

All three cars were approaching a tight bend. Where the fields fell away quickly to a sheer drop thirty metres down to a river.

And Danny's mind went into overdrive.

How many times had he read a book to his dad

where a car was followed, driven alongside, then pushed down a ravine? Dozens. It was one of the most exciting ways of killing people off in crime books. Lots of screeching. Anxious faces. Then the silence before the car smashed on the rocks below.

Since he'd started reading crime books to his dad, Danny had an instinct for danger. Danger that never usually happened.

But this time . . .

Danny looked at Holt. 'That car was definitely in the car park at the pub,' he said. 'No one got out. When we left, it left too. No one got in. Now it's overtaken us. Badly. And it's tailgating Finn. *And* we're about to go round that tight bend over the river.'

'You watch too many films, Danny,' Holt said. But he sounded uneasy. Something in his voice.

'I just have this feeling,' Danny said. 'Can you overtake it? Get in between the Range Rover and Finn's car?'

'Danny. Get real!'

'If you could, would you?'

The Range Rover went right up behind Finn again. Dangerously. Then it dropped back. Leaving a gap.

And – without saying anything more – Holt gunned his engine and accelerated. The Range Rover was still dropping back, so Holt moved past it with ease.

'Happy now?' Holt said, slightly flushed.

Danny nodded. They'd reached the bend. The drop to the river.

'Now what?' Holt asked, looking in his mirror.

Danny looked back. The Range Rover wasn't there.

'Where is it?' Danny shouted.

'There!' Holt said, glancing through his window, his face tight with anxiety.

Danny looked out of the window too. The Range Rover had somehow got alongside them. He caught a face through the black car's tinted window. A fat bald head. A pair of eyes looking daggers at him, as the Range Rover tried to pass.

Then Holt was flashing his lights. On and off a dozen times. Warning Finn.

'What am I doing?' he asked himself.

'I don't know,' Danny shouted. 'But do it!'

The Range Rover had passed them now. Once in front of Holt's car, it slammed its brakes on, forcing Holt to do the same. Then the Range Rover took off, using all of its 400-horsepower to reach Finn's Mercedes ahead. It tried to move alongside Finn. But Finn was going faster, as if he knew something was about to happen, alerted by Holt.

Danny watched the next few seconds in horror.

First the Range Rover moved alongside Finn's car, then it lunged at the Mercedes, forcing Finn to swerve slightly off the road. But they were past the ravine now. Alongside some fields with drystone walls.

Finn tried to get his car back on the road, but his left tyres were caught in the soft grassy verges. Then the Range Rover lunged again, hitting Finn's Mercedes, pitching it flying into a wall, which crumbled, sending huge boulders across the fields, crashing loudly and halting the Mercedes in its tracks.

Holt stopped his car and stared. Danny was already on the phone.

'Ambulance please,' he said. 'And police.'

Holt opened his door and Danny watched him run to the battered Mercedes, his legs disappearing in the long grass.

Danny saw that the black Range Rover had disappeared. He stayed in the car. The road outside was noisy. He knew it was his job to get the ambulance. Holt could see to Finn and Forshaw.

And, anyway, half a dozen cars had stopped now. Men were running across the fields to join Holt.

# *FRIDAY*

## CHANCE OF A LIFETIME

Danny marched into the newspaper offices the next morning. He had to talk to Holt.

After the car crash, Danny was interviewed by the police, then went home. Neither Finn nor Forshaw had been badly hurt. But both were taken to hospital with cuts and bruises. Finn wouldn't play in Moscow: there was no doubt about that.

And that was what had got Danny thinking.

He had spent the evening drawing diagrams, making notes. And going over the questions the police had asked him. Did he see any people get in or out of the Range Rover? Could he tell them exactly where the car had overtaken? Was he *sure* of the number plate – as there was no such number plate on record?

Danny had read a lot about car accidents on the Internet. Especially the death of Diana, Princess of Wales. There were thousands of pages about what could have gone on in the Paris tunnel. Diagrams showing theories of what happened to the car. If it was speeding. If it was involved in a crash with another car. If the driver was drunk. But nobody knew. It was all conjecture.

Whereas witnesses *had* seen the car accident

involving Alex Finn. And the first thing about which Danny was certain: it was *not* an accident.

So then he had asked himself why: why would someone try to injure or kill Alex Finn?

He tried to think of who the suspects could be.

This was one of the techniques he'd learned from reading crime books. Think of who could benefit from the results of a crime. Think of every possibility. Every suspect. Don't rule anything or anyone out. Unless you can be certain.

Danny made a mental list.

A fan of another club who resented him because he'd saved an important shot?

A Russian who hated him for stopping his country winning the night before?

Someone from outside football. An old friend. An ex-girlfriend. A former business partner.

Or someone very much inside of football. A player. Someone he was in competition with. Robert Skatie? Matt McGee? Why not him? He had a dodgy reputation.

A driver he'd cut up? Maybe it was road rage. A stranger.

Or was it nothing to do with Finn? Maybe someone was after Giles Forshaw, the newspaper editor. The passenger in the Mercedes. Not the driver.

Danny wanted to talk to Holt. To find out what he

thought. To start ruling things out. So he could get to the truth.

'Morning, Danny,' Holt said, as Danny knocked and entered his office.

'How's your boss?' Danny asked.

'OK. Back home. He actually shattered his kneecap, so he's in a bit of pain.'

'And Finn?'

'Fine. He's out of hospital too. But his legs are badly bruised. They think he's got ligament damage. He's spending the morning talking to the police.'

'What do *they* say?' Danny asked in an excited voice.

Anton Holt smiled. 'I know what you're up to, Danny. But I think it's best you leave this one to the police.'

'I'm just interested,' Danny said. 'Do they have any theories?'

'None they've told me.'

Danny frowned. Holt was being cagey. So he asked him. Straight out. 'Are you putting it in the paper?'

'The crash? Of course.'

'Not the crash. The black Range Rover.'

Holt paused, then looked down at his desk. 'No,' he said, after a few moments.

'Why not?' Danny said. Too loudly.

Holt softened his voice. 'Right. This is the truth.

I'll tell you once, then we don't talk about it again. OK?'

Danny nodded.

'Giles said not to. He said Alex Finn asked him. As a favour. To keep it quiet. He said it was like Finn was scared of something.'

'Why?'

'I dunno,' Holt said. 'Now we have to leave it.'

'Why?'

'Because it's a secret.'

'But I told the police,' Danny said, 'about the Range Rover.'

'*They've* been asked not to go to the media either,' Holt replied.

Danny frowned. 'Why?'

'Danny. I don't know. Stop asking "Why?"'

'But you can't just sit on it,' Danny protested.

'I'm sorry, Danny. I have to. Those are my orders.'

'Not mine,' Danny said.

Holt put his head in his hands, then looked up.

'Leave it, Danny. Please. Just for now. I promise you: I'll clear this up soon. But not now. It compromises things.'

'Like what?' Danny said. 'So you *do* know stuff. What is it?'

'I can't say.'

'Why not?'

'Danny, leave it. Trust me. There's a good reason we can't do this now. Please.' Holt turned to his laptop.

'Is it something you're writing?' Danny asked.

Holt sighed. He swung his chair round and gave Danny a stern look. 'If I tell you, then no more questions, right?'

'Right,' Danny said.

'Yes. I am writing something.'

'What?'

'I can't say.'

'Why?'

'I just can't, Danny. Don't push me.'

'Why?'

'I'm doing a story. That's all I'm telling you. No more. That's it. Final.'

Danny paused, then nodded. 'OK,' he said. But he was struggling. His thoughts had gathered too much momentum: he wanted to pursue this. But he trusted Holt. And he didn't want to undermine whatever he had going on.

'Anyway,' Holt grinned. 'The police are more interested in this boy who always seems to be around when footballers are kidnapped or crash their cars. They haven't got his name, but . . .'

Danny laughed.

'Listen,' Holt said, once Danny had stopped. 'I've got

an offer for you. It might make up for me . . . for all this.'

Danny frowned. What was this? Was Holt trying to distract him?

Holt leaned over his desk to Danny. 'Giles can't come to Moscow now. His kneecap. So . . .'

Danny's eyes widened.

'. . . I wondered if . . .'

Danny was nodding.

'. . . if you'd like to come in his place.'

'Yes,' Danny said. It was the only word he could get out: he was so excited.

'I mean, we'll have to ask your mum and dad. You'd be away three or four nights.'

'Yes,' Danny said again. 'Yes please.'

Suddenly Danny had been made an offer that was beyond his wildest dreams. His work experience was about to become less and less like work – and more and more like an experience.

'Dad?'

'Danny? Are you OK? Your voice sounds funny.'

'I'm at the *Evening Post*.'

'Is the editor guy OK?' Dad said. 'And Alex Finn?'

'Yeah, they're fine. But I need to ask you something.'

'What?'

'Well, Anton's made me this offer.'

'Right.'

'He's asked if I'd like to go to the Russia game. In Moscow.'

'Right,' his dad said again. But that was all. There was a silence. Danny knew his dad was thinking, that he shouldn't interrupt. However much he wanted to shout 'Pleeeeaaaasssseeee' down the phone.

Eventually his dad spoke. 'Is Anton there?'

'Yeah.'

'Can I talk to him?'

'Yeah.' Danny handed Holt the phone.

Holt paused, then said, 'Hello, Mr Harte. . . . Yes. Moscow. . . . In the press box. Yes. Then a hotel. The President. Very posh. And secure. It's the one the team are staying in. It's owned by the government, so it's the safest in Russia.'

Danny's mouth gaped open. The team hotel. *And* the team flight.

'Sunday,' Holt said. 'First thing . . . Thursday morning. Back in England about midday.'

Danny was trying to put the conversation together, imagining what his dad was saying. What Anton's answers meant.

'Yes,' Holt said. 'Very much part of his work experience . . . OK.' He handed Danny the handset.

Danny grabbed it and spoke breathlessly. 'Dad?'

'I need to talk to your mum,' Dad said. 'I'll call her at work, then call you back. OK?'

'Yeah. Thanks, Dad.'

Danny leafed through the day's papers. All about the day before. The life-threatening crash suffered by the footballer. But no theories why it could have happened.

An accident. That was it. The police were investigating, but were not looking for anyone else in connection with the crash.

Danny's mind was all over the place. He was thinking about the crash, but also the trip to Russia. Would or wouldn't he be allowed to go? It was so important.

He glanced at Holt answering emails on his laptop, looking like today was a day like any other.

Waiting for Dad to call back was doing Danny's head in.

'Anton?'

'Yep.'

'What are you writing about?'

'What?' Holt said, preoccupied.

'Are you writing about the crash?'

'The crash?'

'Yeah.' Danny knew he'd promised not to ask any more about it. But he couldn't just sit quiet with an unanswered question in his head.

'Some nutter wanting to cut up a flash car, I reckon,' Holt said in a deadpan voice, like he didn't mean what he said.

Danny frowned. 'There was more to it than that. They waited for us to leave the car park.'

'I reckon that was a coincidence, Danny,' Holt said. 'Listen. We've talked about this.'

And for the first time since he'd known Holt, Danny felt that the reporter wasn't treating him like an equal. Maybe even treating him like a kid.

Danny looked him in the eye. Holt looked away first.

Then the phone rang.

Holt picked it up. Then nodded.

'Danny, it's something ... you know ... do you mind just sitting outside for a minute?'

Danny nodded. Holt had done this before. They'd agreed that Danny would leave the room if Holt was having a conversation that was off the record or sensitive. Danny wasn't bothered about that. But he was bothered that the call wasn't from his dad. He really wanted his *dad* to call. To say, yes, he could go to Moscow.

Outside Holt's office, Danny read some more newspapers. Holt had insisted he read not just other sports pages, but the news too. He said Danny needed to know about more than football. He needed to know what was happening in the countries where football was going on.

Were there wars? Was there poverty? Was there a lot of corruption?

To understand football, Holt had said, you needed to understand the world.

Danny sat down to read *The Times*.

Railway workers on strike.

More trouble in the Middle East.

Boys not reading as much as girls.

Then a story about Russia.

**RUSSIAN FOOTBALL FANATIC TUPOLEV IN GAS COUP**

**The Russian billionaire and football impresario Dmitri Tupolev has been in talks with governments in Hungary, Bulgaria and Serbia, to finalize the route for his gas pipeline, running from Russia to Western Europe. Reports suggest he will seal a contract with all three countries to deliver gas to the West for the next fifty years.**

**Tupolev, who owns 51% of Gasprospekt, also owns 100% of the top football clubs in Ukraine and Russia. It is very much anticipated that he will move soon for a club in Spain, Italy or England.**

*Another English club owned by someone from abroad*, Danny thought. This worried him. Whenever outside investors came in and bought a football club, the fans always lost out. They were charged more. Some could no longer afford to get in the stadium their family had gone to for generations.

Danny looked up to see Anton waving at him through the glass wall of his office, holding his phone out to Danny.

'It's your dad,' Holt mouthed, grinning.

Danny went back into Holt's office, breathed in and took the phone.

'Dad?'

'Danny?'

'Yeah.'

'I've talked to your mum,' his dad said.

'Yeah?'

'About Russia.'

'Right?' said Danny, getting impatient.

'Do you want to know what she said?' Dad said.

Danny said nothing. He waited. His dad was doing this on purpose: winding him up.

'Are you still there, Danny?'

'Come on, Dad,' Danny said. 'You're doing my head in.'

'Danny.'

'Yes?'

'You can go to Moscow.'

Danny punched the air.

## *THE GAMBLE*

The telephone rang dead on midday. Just as Kenneth Francis had expected. He had no doubts about who was calling. Again. This time he let it ring for a few moments: he didn't want the person at the other end to think he was at his beck and call.

After four rings he answered.

'Dmitri? How are you?'

'Good. And are you having news for me?'

Kenneth Francis smiled. There was no messing about with Dmitri Tupolev. He wanted answers.

Francis paused again, glancing round the study in his yacht. Dark oak bookshelves holding twenty metres of the world's greatest books. He knew the exact measurements because he had ordered the books *by* the metre. Not by the book. He was, in fact, proud to say that he'd not read one of them. They were all in mint condition.

'I do have news,' Francis said eventually.

'Then Alex Finn is dead? This is –'

'Not dead,' Francis interrupted. He knew he had to handle this well. The future of his relationship with this Russian – and therefore his own future – depended on it.

'*Not* dead?' Tupolev said in a cold tone.

'Alex Finn suffered a car accident yesterday, Dmitri. He will be out of football for a long time. And, of course, he is very scared.'

'*Not* dead?' Tupolev repeated, as if he wanted to hear a different reply from what he had just been told.

This was the moment Kenneth Francis had to strike. The most important speech of his life.

'No, not dead,' he said firmly. 'If he were dead, the English police would launch an investigation into a serious murder, rather than merely logging another car accident. If he were dead, the game on Wednesday would be called off, ruining our plans. If he were dead, the English police would get to the bottom of it, I promise you.'

Francis paused in case Tupolev wanted to interject. But the Russian was silent. This, Francis knew, could be a good sign. Or a bad one. And he knew he had to gamble.

'Frankly, Dmitri, the police in England are much more thorough than they are in your country. Mainly because they are not told what to do by the likes of me – or you. And here, also, we do not need to kill people to –' Francis tried to find the right words – 'influence their behaviour.'

Francis stopped speaking. He had said his piece.

He wanted to hear what Tupolev had to say now, to see if the gamble had paid off.

There was a short silence.

Then an explosion of laughter.

Over two thousand kilometres away from the laughter, Francis smiled. He knew he had said the right thing. He had been direct with the Russian. Rude about his country. But it had worked. Dmitri Tupolev truly was into plain speaking.

Then the Russian spoke. 'So, what will you do to speak to the other goalkeepers? McGee? Skatie? For me ... is clear ... I mean important ... that Russia beats England on Wednesday. It will happen.'

Francis smiled again.

'It is McGee we need to think about, Dmitri.'

'Not Robert Skatie?'

'No, McGee will play.'

'And what do you –'

'Matt McGee is an interesting man, Dmitri,' Francis said. 'I have had a man looking into him for me. A private investigator.'

'And what did he find?' Tupolev said.

'That Matt McGee is a man with a past. And a present.' Francis paused for effect.

But Tupolev said nothing.

So Francis went on. 'In the past he was involved with some unsavoury characters.'

'Unsavoury?' Tupolev said. 'What does this mean? That he was sweet? How can he be sweet?'

Francis held back a laugh. 'No,' he said. 'Unsavoury means bad, criminal.'

'Tell me more.'

'There are links to counterfeit money. And to drugs. And other crimes.'

'You are proposing blackmail?'

'Yes,' Francis said. 'But there's more. I have made it my business to find out that Matt McGee is in severe debt. He gambles.'

'Gambles?'

'Bets. He bets money on anything that moves.'

'And you are recommending?'

Francis stopped to think. He often wondered how good Tupolev's English was. Sometimes he used words like 'recommending' and 'blackmail', but would then struggle with words like 'gamble'. A word he should know better than any other.

Francis knew he had to be careful. He should not forget that this man was one of the most dangerous in the world.

'A two-pronged attack,' Francis said. 'One: we threaten to expose his past. Two: we say we will pay all his gambling debts.'

'To pay?' Tupolev spat. 'Let us just kill him. Pay him? This is one thing we do not do in Russia.'

Francis spoke calmly. 'We will not pay him, Dmitri. You misunderstand. We will *say* that we will pay him.'

Again, after a pause, Francis heard Tupolev's raucous laughter. It was a good sign. A very good sign. They could move forward. Francis had failed to finish off Alex Finn. But everything was still on track.

# SPIES EVERYWHERE

Anton Holt gave Danny the afternoon off.

'Find your passport,' he said. 'Text me its number. Someone here will sort your visa. Then get some roubles and some thermal underwear. OK?'

Danny went home. His dad found his passport and Danny texted the number through to Holt. Then Danny asked his dad if he wanted to come to the Post Office to get some roubles. As for the thermal underwear, Danny didn't bother. There was no way he was wearing anything ridiculous like that. He'd rather freeze.

'Now?' Dad said.

'Yeah. If they don't have any in I'll need to order them. For tomorrow morning, Anton said.'

They walked down to the shops together. Danny's dad next to him, just on his shoulder. Along streets of terraced houses, through leafier roads, past a church. Danny was still amazed at his dad. How could he walk without a stick, without holding Danny's arm, just following his voice or his footsteps?

'So what do you know about Russia?' Dad said, interrupting Danny's thoughts.

Danny was about to reply, but his dad cut in.

'I can't believe you – how jammy can you get? First you get invited to the European Championships. And now you're off to a World Cup qualifier.'

'I'm just lucky,' Danny said, stopping to cross the road at the lights.

'Hmmmm,' Dad said, stopping too. 'Maybe you are. But just make sure you stay out of trouble on this trip. You know what I mean?'

Danny felt like his dad was glaring at him through his dark glasses, but he knew he couldn't be.

'All I know,' Danny said, 'to answer your previous question, is that Russia isn't as bad as it used to be. We did it in history last year, remember? The Cold War and all that.'

'The Cold War *and all that*?' Dad mimicked Danny. 'Do you know, before my accident, all I used to read were thrillers about the Cold War *and all that*? I was obsessed. Everyone was. They were spying on us. We were spying on them. They were the communists: we were the free world. They had enough bombs aimed at us to sink the whole island. And everyone was always saying "The Russians are coming!"'

'Coming where?'

Danny asked the questions as they crossed the road, towards the row of shops on the high street.

'To invade us.'

'Us?'

'Yes.'

'Why us?'

'Because they had all these tanks and bombs and they wanted to come get us. Make us communist too.'

'And did they?' Danny asked. 'I mean, did they really want to do that?'

'No. I don't suppose so. It was a funny time. Anyone going to Russia was immediately watched and suspected by both sides. The British *and* the Russians.' Dad stopped walking. 'You've seen *Spooks* on TV, right?'

'Yeah. The MI5 thing?'

'And you know how it's all about al-Qaida – the enemy?'

'Yeah.'

'Well, there was no al-Qaida then. Not in the seventies and eighties. It was the Russians. The papers were full of it. And the books.'

'Right,' Danny said.

'Are we in front of the café?' Dad asked.

His dad was spot on. That's exactly where they were.

'Yeah,' Danny said.

'You go and get your roubles,' Dad said. 'I'll get the teas in.'

'Can I have a Coke?' Danny asked.

Dad waved his hand and pushed the door of the

café open. Danny walked another fifty yards and went into the Post Office.

The Post Office was a large square room with three counters at the far end. There were two racks of shelves in the middle of the room, with kids' toys, stationery and gift cards on display. Two of the counters were busy. The third was free. The man behind it already had his eyes on Danny. He was bald, sixty-plus and was wearing glasses.

'Yes, sir?' he said.

Danny had been served by this man dozens of times. Getting stamps for his mum. Posting parcels for his dad. But he still called Danny 'sir'.

'Can I have some roubles, please?' Danny asked.

'Roubles?' The man raised an eyebrow.

'Yes, Russian –'

'I know where roubles are from, sir,' the man said, utterly deadpan.

Danny nodded.

'I'll have to phone the order through,' the man said.

'When will they come?' Danny said. 'I need them for –'

'Tomorrow, sir?'

'Great.' Danny smiled.

The man eyed Danny, then turned his back. He dialled a number. Waited. Then he turned to face Danny through the glass screen. 'Business or pleasure?'

Danny didn't know what to say.

'Business or pleasure?' the man repeated in the same tone.

'I'm not sure,' Danny said.

'I see. Let's say pleasure, shall we? Do you have anything to do when you're there? They'll want to know.'

'OK,' Danny said. He felt nervous. Who were *they*? The people on the other end of the phone. Why did they want to ask all these questions?

'Pleasure,' Danny said eventually.

'How much?' the man asked.

'How much what?'

'Money.'

'A hundred pounds, please.'

The man raised his eyebrow again.

'That won't get you very far,' the man said. 'Are you going on your own?'

Danny felt like telling the man everything, but decided not to. He'd give short answers now.

'No.'

The man nodded. 'I see,' he said.

Danny tried to hear what the man said on the phone. But he couldn't catch a word. The man was behind the glass screen, a few metres away, his back turned. Thoughts flashed through Danny's mind. Why all the questions? Did it matter if he was there for business or pleasure? Did the man really need to phone someone?

His mind drifted to what his dad had said.

*Anyone going to Russia was immediately watched and suspected by both sides. The British and the Russians.*

Danny wondered if the Post Office man was phoning someone other than the money people. Maybe he already had a load of roubles and was phoning to alert the authorities that there was a boy going to Russia and that he only wanted a hundred pounds. Someone needed to keep an eye on him. Someone needed to check him out. Someone needed to *spy* on him.

'Tomorrow morning?'

'What?' Danny was surprised. The man was facing him, the phone down.

'Tomorrow morning. Your roubles.'

'That's great. Thank you.'

'You're welcome, sir.'

Once Danny had paid, he left the Post Office quickly. He noticed that the man behind the counter was eyeing him over his glasses – all the way out until he was on the pavement. Then he thought he saw the man smile.

Dad was sitting in the corner on his own. A cup of tea and a can of Coke in front of him. The café was full of noise. Conversations between people and a radio on in the background.

Danny sat opposite him.

'Did you get them?' Dad said.

'Tomorrow,' Danny replied.

'No trouble?'

'No, but . . .' Danny paused. 'I felt like the guy at the Post Office was monitoring me or something.'

'Who? Frank?'

'The bald guy with the glasses. He's . . .' Danny stopped. Even *he* made the mistake of describing what people looked like to his dad.

'That's Frank,' Dad said.

'About sixty?'

'Sixty-four,' Dad said. 'I knew him well before the accident. I know what he looks like. We were mates. Sort of. He would have been having some fun with you.'

'Right,' Danny said.

'What did he say?'

'It's not what he said. He was just funny,' Danny said. 'He was making me feel like I was doing something suspicious.'

'He was winding you up,' Dad said, laughing.

'You reckon?'

'He knows all about Russia, does Frank.'

'Yeah?' Somehow Danny wasn't surprised.

'Frank was a member of the Communist Party when he was younger,' Dad told him.

'What does that mean?'

'He was a communist. He wanted to overthrow the rich and share the money out. To put it simply.'

Danny stared at his dad. 'You're kidding.' He drank his Coke quickly. It was cold and felt good.

'Danny?' Dad said.

'Yeah?'

'Is it going well with Anton? At the paper, I mean. Do you like the job?'

'It's great. I love it,' Danny said. He could feel an important question coming on. His dad did this: asked him an easy question to move towards something more serious he wanted to know.

'So do you reckon you'd prefer it,' Dad said, 'to being a detective?'

Danny was shocked his dad could think that. 'No way,' he said.

'Right,' Dad replied, muted.

'I mean,' Danny said. 'There's things that are the same. You have to find stuff out. You have to put it all together. So I suppose it's not all that different. But I'm still going to be a detective.'

Dad nodded. 'Will you do me a favour in Moscow, then?'

Danny frowned. 'Sure,' he said. He was right: something was coming. And this wasn't going to be a request for him to bring back a Russian doll.

'Don't be a detective out there. OK?'

'OK,' Danny said.

'It's different in Russia,' Dad went on. 'Even now. I mean, we're not sworn enemies any more. But it's a very different world. Frankly, some of the police are corrupt. There are a lot of criminal gangs. Mafia.'

Dad stopped talking: Danny had gone quiet.

'I'm not trying to scare you, Danny. If you're there as a tourist – as a football fan, as a boy – you'll be fine. Just be careful. This is a great opportunity for you. An amazing thing to happen. So long as you stay close to Anton and do what normal boys do, you'll be fine. OK?'

Danny nodded.

Deep down, though, he was beginning to feel nervous. Or was he excited? He wasn't sure which.

# SATURDAY

## HOUSE PARTY

'So tell us again,' Charlotte said.

Danny had been daydreaming. About the man at the Post Office. When Danny had gone in there that morning to collect his roubles, his dad's friend had passed him the money and whispered, 'Don't forget to dust a bit of chalk on to your suitcase – to make sure it's not been tampered with.' Danny knew it was a joke. But it had set his mind racing. Was it going to be like that in Russia? He felt like he was about to step into the pages of a spy novel.

'What?' Danny asked, knowing that Charlotte had spoken, but not what she had said.

'About the Range Rover,' Charlotte said.

Danny was sitting outside a house that backed on to the school grounds. Inside the house a party was going on. Here in the garden Charlotte and Paul were quizzing him. The sky was darkening as they looked across the playing fields.

'I've said. It was waiting at the car park when we left. It followed Alex Finn's car. Then it overtook me and Anton. Then it forced Finn off the road.'

'So why,' Charlotte asked, 'was it not on the news?

All it said was that he'd come off the road on a notorious bend. And that it was an accident.'

Danny shrugged. 'I'm just telling you what I saw.'

'And why doesn't that Anton bloke write something about it?'

'I dunno.' Danny felt guilty not saying, but he knew he should say nothing.

'Yeah, right!' Charlotte said.

It was getting cooler. Lights were coming on in houses in the street. The others who'd been talking outside had gone in. Music was hammering out of the house, loud and hard. Danny had spotted faces at the lit windows.

'And suddenly you're just heading off to Moscow,' Charlotte said. 'Just like that.'

'Yeah,' Danny said defensively.

'Sure.'

'What?'

'Danny. Don't tell me there's nothing going on.'

'There's nothing going on,' Danny said, deadpan.

'It's to do with last time,' Paul cut in, 'isn't it?'

'Last time?'

'Sam Roberts. Gawthorpe. All that.'

'It's not,' Danny protested.

'All I know,' Charlotte said, 'is that you're up to something.'

And then Danny found he was laughing. He was the

one who was always accused of seeing crime around every corner: now *they* were making up things that might not be there.

When Danny had stopped laughing, Charlotte went on. 'Here's how I see it. Four months ago you were involved in saving Sam Roberts from kidnappers. But there was nothing on the news. And you swore us to secrecy. And now you're there when Alex Finn is nearly killed in a car accident. And – what do you know? – it's not on the news. Even though you say it wasn't an accident. And – to add to that – you're off to see England play in Moscow.'

Danny nodded. It was all true. He could see Charlotte and Paul watching him, grinning. He knew why they thought what they thought. And their theories were so exciting he wished they were true. But the truth *was* that there was nothing going on. Not with him, anyway. Not for sure, but he wondered if he *should* tell them about his half-baked theories. Why not? They'd kept the Roberts stuff to themselves. He trusted them.

'Look, it's all straightforward,' he said, 'it's only . . .'

'Here we go,' Charlotte said to Paul.

Danny lowered his voice. 'It's just I think the accident wasn't an accident. That's all. I think someone tried to kill Alex Finn.'

'Who?' Paul asked.

'I don't know.'

'Great detective you are,' Charlotte smiled.

'There's a number of things it could be,' Danny said.

'Like?'

'Well, someone had to have a reason to do it.'

'Obviously,' Charlotte agreed.

'So who?' Danny asked.

'Like I told you, you're the wannabe detective,' she said.

'Well, it could be another player,' Danny said.

'Matt McGee,' Paul cut in.

'Why him?'

'He's well dodgy.'

'And Skatie isn't?'

'No,' Paul said.

'Fair enough. So it could be McGee. But why? Could it be someone else? Who else would have a reason?'

'Someone Russian,' Paul said. 'Revenge for last week.'

'Yeah, but that's an extreme reaction,' Charlotte pointed out. 'No one would try to kill a player of another team – just for beating *their* team.'

'Maybe,' Danny said. 'Maybe *not*. Unless there's more to it than just a football result.'

'Like what?' Paul wanted to know.

'I don't know.'

'Great,' Charlotte said, rolling her eyes.

Danny looked at Charlotte. Why was she always on his case like this? Always wanting an argument.

'Who else?' Danny said, pushing them.

'A bookmaker?' Paul suggested.

'Could be.'

'Why are you asking us?' Charlotte said. '*You're* the one who goes to court cases, reads the crime pages in the paper, films burglars, puts newspaper clippings and maps up on his bedroom walls.'

'Three heads are better than one,' Danny said. And he meant it. He loved talking to these two about his investigations. If you could bounce ideas off other people they could help you work out what was true and what was a mistake. That's why he was doing it. He remembered a crime novel he'd read to his dad. Based in Sweden. The main detective used to talk to his colleagues, trying out ideas, letting them rubbish his theories. Until he found the answer.

'So you reckon McGee,' Paul said. 'I do.'

'I dunno,' Danny said. 'I've read some interesting stuff about him on the Net.'

'Like what?'

'Like he's involved with all sorts. In fact,' Danny paused, 'I saw him with that drug dealer a few weeks ago. In the city centre. The one who was on trial.'

'There you go then,' Paul declared.

'Yeah, but that's not enough.'

'Who was the criminal?' Charlotte said.

'Gavin Barnes,' Danny said.

*'Excuse me?'*

Danny looked at Charlotte. Who'd said that?

*'EXCUSE ME?'*

The voice had come from over the fence. It was a tall woman. Her posh voice piercing the night.

'Hello,' Charlotte said.

'Could you tell your friends inside that if the music is not turned down in one minute I am going to call the police?' The voice paused. 'Please.'

'OK,' Charlotte said, smiling and getting up, leaving the woman behind the fence to utter murmurs of surprise rather than annoyance.

Danny grinned at Paul. He liked Charlotte: the way she always surprised people.

Seconds later the volume of the music dropped. And Charlotte emerged. The woman nodded and said thank you. Quietly.

'One more thing,' Charlotte said to Danny on her return.

'What?'

'I want you to send me a video of yourself every day you're in Moscow.'

'Why?'

'Evidence,' Charlotte said.

'Evidence of what?'

'Evidence that you're OK.'

# *SUNDAY*

## *FEAR OF FLYING*

It was a British Airways Boeing 737. Danny studied the plane through the huge panes of glass of Terminal One.

Here he was again.

Every time he was about to get on a plane he had the same question: how the hell could something so huge and heavy – filled with people, bags and aviation fuel – fly?

He knew he'd never understand it.

He smiled, checking his pocket to make sure his passport and roubles were still there.

So far there had been no sign of the England squad. Holt had come with Danny through to the airport lounge, then gone off to a café to do some emails on his laptop. And Danny was left to contemplate being on a plane with England's finest footballers, several FA officials and most of the country's leading football writers.

He was nervous. Or excited. He wasn't sure which. He'd felt like this since he'd left home.

Even Emily hadn't been able to put a dampener on him. When Dad had handed him a book as a present for the trip, his sister had demanded a present from Russia. She'd asked for a Russian doll: she'd always wanted a set, she said. Danny had raised his eyebrows at her, then shook his head.

The lounge for gate thirteen – all comfy orange seats and coffee shops – was full of football writers. A group of men in suits, without ties. Some talking. Many into their mobile phones. Danny recognized some of them from the newspapers; at the top of most sports columns, nowadays, there was a small postage stamp-sized picture of the writer. Then Danny saw Gary Lineker. And Mark Lawrenson. He grinned, then looked at the floor, trying not to stare.

But it was when the players arrived that things got exciting. All twenty-two walking together. All twenty-two in blue suits *with* ties. Danny knew why this was. The England manager demanded the players dress to represent their country. In team colours on and off the pitch.

Danny recognized all of the players.

Peter Day, Ipswich.

Stuart Lane, Aston Villa.

Patrick Bingley, Arsenal.

Phil White, Liverpool.

Mike Leigh, Reading.

Lewis Poole, Leeds United.

He regretted that Sam Roberts was not among

them. He'd got to know Roberts a bit after the kidnapping. Roberts had even been to his house for tea.

As the team arrived, the whole airport lounge went quiet for a few seconds. All you could hear was their footsteps. It reminded Danny of a church, when the choir and vicars come through the congregation. And then someone shouted 'Good luck, lads!' And suddenly there were lots of voices calling out.

A man at the front of the players ushered the team through to the plane immediately. He handed the flight official a pile of passports. And the players just walked through the business-class entrance – and disappeared.

When they'd gone Danny looked back at the lounge. Hundreds of people hanging over balconies and stairways, huddled in groups. All staring.

On the plane there was no sign of the players.

'Where are they?' Danny asked Holt, who was clipping his seat-belt across his lap.

'Business class. Up front,' Holt said. 'Beyond those curtains.'

'Can't you talk to them during the flight? Do interviews?'

'Rarely,' Holt said. 'And only usually at press conferences. And only with an FA official there. Even in the hotel we've got to be careful. Not talk about the team and tactics and all that. We'd be banned. But things are better than they used to be. Apparently under one former English manager, you couldn't get near anyone.'

The plane began to move. In reverse. Then it taxied towards the runway. Danny was by the window, with Holt next to him in the aisle.

A hand came over the top of the seat and tapped Holt on the head.

'Hold on tight, Anton,' a voice said. 'I hear this captain's a bit ropey.'

Holt grinned and looked back. 'Cheers, David,' he said. 'That's a great help.'

The hand disappeared, followed by laughter.

'What was that about?' Danny said.

'Flying,' Holt said.

'What about it?'

'Nothing.'

'What?' Danny insisted.

'I'm not keen,' Holt said. 'That's all.'

'Really?' Danny said. 'I love it.'

'Well, you enjoy it,' Holt muttered, closing his eyes.

Danny shrugged and stared out of the window. He loved this bit. He'd been on planes six times in his life. To Italy and back. Florida. And Cyprus.

The plane stopped at the end of the runway. Over

the intercom the captain said, 'Crew prepare for take-off' in a low and confident voice.

Then the engines began to roar.

Danny was pushed back into his seat. He watched the airport move by as the plane accelerated. The noise was thrilling. The speed faster and faster. They must be halfway down the runway now. This was the point Danny loved. Unable to believe the plane would take off. But knowing it was going too fast to stop now. Then feeling the lift. The jump of the plane. Then the dramatic upsurge into the sky, the airport and the roads and fields around it suddenly falling away. He felt his stomach cramp as the undercarriage banged shut.

Danny looked at Holt. His eyes were shut tight, lines across his face. Danny had wanted to ask him about the car crash. But this was probably not a good time. He laughed to himself.

Danny watched the airport and the city become smaller and smaller. Lines of cars on motorways. Reservoirs reflecting the clouds. Sunlight filling the cabin as they passed over England.

He loved flying.

A few minutes later, Holt was asleep. So Danny took out the book his dad had given him. *The Spy Who Came in from the Cold*. He got straight into it: a spy wants to stop being a spy. But he is dragged into events in Communist East Germany, where he doesn't know who to trust. His friend turns out to be his enemy. His enemy turns out to be his friend. Double agents turn out to be merely agents. Agents, double agents.

Danny settled back and began to read.

## *DOUBLE AGENT*

After about half an hour, a team of cabin crew brought trays of food around. Danny put his book down.

He looked at his food. Cottage pie. Limp vegetables. Sponge cake. A carton of water.

Holt seemed happier now he'd had a short sleep. He smiled at Danny.

'Good?' he said, eyeing Danny's food.

'Not bad,' Danny said.

'And you're looking forward to Moscow?'

'Sort of,' Danny replied. This was the moment he'd been waiting for. To get Holt to talk about the crash.

'Sort of?'

'I want to talk about the other day,' Danny said. 'The accident.'

'Leave it, Danny,' Holt said, his voice quieter. 'Please!'

'How can we?' Danny whispered.

'I mean *you*, Danny. Just enjoy the trip. I've responsibilities to keep you out of trouble. To your parents. Remember I promised you'd be fine. That I'd look after you?'

Danny knew now that there was definitely something

going on. More than Holt just writing a story. Why was he being so cagey? He'd always been straight before.

And an insane thought drifted into Danny's mind.

Holt.

Was *he* a double agent? Someone who worked for two sides. Maybe *he* was involved in something more than writing newspaper articles.

But Danny knew he was being stupid. The book he'd been reading was warping his thoughts. Holt was his friend. Holt was straight. If he was hiding anything it was to *protect* Danny.

But Danny just couldn't leave it alone.

'You're treating me like a kid,' he said. He regretted it immediately.

'That's way out of order,' Holt whispered loudly. 'I have never treated you like a kid. What about Sam Roberts? I trusted you all the way with that. Remember?'

Danny nodded. He had to concede that point. It was true.

'So don't accuse me of that,' Holt went on.

'Tell me *some*thing,' Danny pleaded.

'I'll tell you one thing, Danny. And this is the last thing I'll say. Otherwise you're going back to England on this plane once it reaches Moscow.'

Danny's shoulders dropped. 'What?'

'Leave it well alone. Enjoy the trip – but no funny

business. And that is the last I have to say on it. If anything, you're *making* me treat you like a kid by *behaving* like a kid. OK?'

Holt held Danny with a fierce stare.

'OK,' Danny said, reluctantly.

It was a closed door. Danny tried not to feel the sort of frustrated anger he felt towards his parents when they told him off. Because that was what had just happened.

An hour later – somewhere over Poland – Danny was waiting outside the plane toilet. In the space between business class and economy. Bursting. The cabin crew had brought him three cans of Coke already.

He tried to take his mind off it by looking around the plane. At the small oval windows. At the seats, row after row, going back to the tail of the plane. But he couldn't stop hopping from one foot to another. Until he heard a voice behind him.

'You all right?'

Danny turned round.

It was Matt McGee. *The* Matt McGee.

Danny had nothing to say. Here was the man he'd been thinking about, almost investigating.

'You're a bit young for press, aren't you?' McGee went on. He was tall – like Finn – but had darker hair and a more friendly face.

Danny grinned. 'I'm on – er – work experience. With Anton Holt.'

McGee stepped back. 'You're kidding,' he said. 'When I was a kid I did work experience at a supermarket. Unbelievable.'

'I was lucky,' Danny said.

'So what are your mates doing for their work experience? Is one of them flying this plane?' McGee grabbed on to one of the seats, like he was worried they were going to crash.

Danny laughed.

Then the toilet door opened. Danny recognized the man emerging from the small room. Ray Stubbs from *Match of the Day*. Stubbs nodded to McGee.

'After you,' McGee said to Danny.

And Danny locked himself in the toilet. He put his back against the door. To get his breath back. He'd talked to Matt McGee. And he'd seemed all right. A really nice man. Not the drunken, gambling, former criminal everyone made him out to be.

## WEIRD CITY

The first thing that struck Danny in the airport was the signs. Half the letters in the words were weird – not from the A to Z alphabet he knew. There were back-to-front Ns and upside-down Vs. It was seriously unsettling. Danny liked to know what signs said.

All the press and FA officials had to queue in a line to have their visas checked. Along with Danny. But the players had gone on, whisked away by the man with his pile of passports.

As Danny approached passport control he began to feel nervous. There were several glass booths. Each had a stern-faced official checking the passengers through. Danny saw what they did. They looked at the passport, then at the person's face. After putting the passport through some sort of scanner, they then spent a long time reading it.

Behind them was a row of police or army officers. Each with a huge brimmed hat. And – Danny was shocked to see – they carried machine-guns. He'd never seen a machine-gun before: not in real life.

There was a line on the floor you had to stand behind before you were summoned. Danny dutifully stood behind it. Then *he* was summoned. By a woman. About the same age as his mum. Her dark hair pinned back severely so that it pulled her eyebrows upwards with a look of surprise. Her eyes were narrow, her nose long and thin.

She looked at Danny's passport. Then at his face.

Danny knew he had to try and look like himself. He didn't want to smile. You weren't supposed to smile.

Then she scanned his passport through her machine. And passed it back to him.

He was surprised how quick it had been. But he didn't hang around to complain.

Danny walked on. Past the machine-guns. As fast as he could without running. He wanted to find Holt. Quickly. Where *was* he? Everything was glass panes and white panelling. It was featureless, putting Danny on edge. All the time he was thinking that security would be on the look-out for people behaving strangely. And now he couldn't help but think that *he* was behaving strangely.

Danny looked back for Holt, but was quickly told – in hand gestures – to move on, by one of the machine-gunners.

So he kept walking, down a corridor, through a hall, a string of people passing ahead of and behind him.

Where was he going?

Where was Holt?

He was starting to wish Holt *had* put him back on

the plane. He felt out of his depth. And all he was doing was walking through an airport. What would he be like in the city? At the football stadium?

He came to another corridor. Two automatic doors opened to let him through. There was a blur of faces. Signs. Colour. Light.

Danny went to stand at the side of what was clearly the arrivals hall. He'd wait there.

He walked through a cluster of men, each offering him a taxi, in English. He shook his head. He wanted to say '*Nyet*' but worried that 'no' alone sounded rude. Not knowing how to say 'No, thank you', he preferred to shake his head. One of the taxi-drivers smiled at him – as if he understood.

With time to spare, Danny took out his phone, set up the video and – holding the phone in front of him – began to film the airport. The strange alphabet. The strange hats on the soldiers. The people.

He'd promised Charlotte a video diary. This would be his first entry.

Danny ended his film and sent it to Charlotte. Then he was relieved to see Holt coming over to him, smiling.

If Danny had looked up at that moment, through the glass sides of Moscow's Domodedovo International Airport, he'd have seen a small private plane banking right to head over the city.

Inside the plane were two men. Dmitri Tupolev, Russian oligarch and football enthusiast. And a UK citizen, now known as Kenneth Francis, City trader.

The inside of the private plane was spectacular. The main cabin was taken up by a large dining table, made of dark shining wood. Each of the men sat in a huge leather chair, which swivelled to face either of two giant TV screens. At one end was a doorway. Francis had already been through it, past a sprawling double bed, into a bathroom with a huge mirror, shower and sink. All – Francis suspected – with gold fittings. Real gold.

The private plane was heading for a small airstrip adjacent to a large country estate and several thousand acres of wild land, stocked with deer, boar and salmon. Tupolev's private hunting estate, fifty kilometres east of Russia's capital.

Both men were drinking champagne, served by a tall blonde woman in a smart black skirt and top. Francis was stunned by her beauty.

He was trying to keep calm. Although he was a rich man, used to power and wealth, the man who had met him at the airport was in a different league. Dmitri Tupolev was worth somewhere near six billion dollars. He was one of the richest men in Russia.

Francis was impressed by his clothes. A perfect suit in the finest materials. A crisp white shirt. And an enormously expensive tie. His shoes were long and thin, and made from shining crocodile skin.

But the man inside the fancy clothes looked tired. Compared to the pictures Francis had seen of him. And slightly cross. As a result he looked like a man you should not disappoint.

'I have created an opportunity to speak to Matt McGee,' Tupolev said to Francis.

'Good,' Francis said. He was again impressed with Tupolev's use of English.

'I have invited the England players, the press and Football Association officials to a reception. Tomorrow. At my dacha . . . my country retreat.'

'Excellent. And did they accept?'

Tupolev looked at Francis like he was an idiot. 'Yes. Of course,' he said.

'Good. Then we can talk to McGee.'

Tupolev leaned across and summoned the woman in black, indicating their champagne glasses were nearly empty. She came quickly and filled them both. Tupolev nodded and patted the woman on the leg as she passed.

'Tonight we will dine at my dacha,' Tupolev exclaimed. 'Tomorrow I will show you some of my . . . properties . . . in Moscow. My hotel. Yes?'

'Yes,' Francis replied.

'You have the portfolio?' Tupolev said once the woman had moved away.

Francis nodded. He handed Tupolev a thin file.

'I have highlighted the main issues, as we discussed,' Francis said. 'McGee's history. His links with criminal gangs in his youth. The counterfeit scam that I am confident he was involved in. Also, a record of his gambling activity in the last two years. His debts, as you can see, are . . .' Francis paused. How could he call debts of £950,000 'huge' to a man who had far more than that? He searched for the right words: '. . . a problem for him.'

Tupolev nodded. 'Yes,' he said, 'this is excellent. We can use this. And you think he will do as we want? You think he will accept the money?'

'I think we should offer to wipe out his debts. Then, if he is not keen, talk to him about his past.'

Tupolev guffawed. 'Yes,' he said. 'Then, if that doesn't work, let us talk to him about his future.'

Francis smiled at the man lounging on the other side of the plane. He knew what Tupolev meant. And he didn't like the idea. He hoped they could stop short of murder.

# MOSCOW

Danny sat on the bed in his hotel room and gazed around it in awe. The room was huge. The bed was huge. The mirror on the wall was huge. And through the huge window – seventeen floors up – he could see the city stretching into the distance. Churches. Statues. The river wide and long.

The TV was on when he came into the room. There was a message:

WELCOME THE PRESIDENT HOTEL, MR HARTE. PLEASE TO PHONE RECEPTION IF THE NEED FOR HELP ARISES.

Danny smiled and took a photo of the screen with his phone.

Then he noticed he'd had a reply from Charlotte. His heart skipped a beat when he saw her name.

Why did she always make him feel like that?

He read the text:

**Thx 4 vid. Cn't u send anything more exciting? :-) C xxx**

*

Yes, he could. He would. Because Moscow wasn't like other cities he knew. There was something about it. It felt different. He wondered if it was all the stories his dad had told him. Or the things he'd read in books about spies and the KGB.

For one thing, he definitely felt like he was being watched.

But how could he put a feeling like that into a video for Charlotte? He had absolutely no idea.

Danny jumped when his hotel room phone rang.

He wondered, before he picked it up, if the phone was tapped. In fact, it occurred to him that there could be a camera in the room. In the TV maybe. Or hidden in one of the fifteen light fittings. Maybe someone had seen him taking photos? Maybe someone had intercepted his texts? Or even his thoughts?

Danny smiled. He was being paranoid again. Trying to make his life more exciting, as if he was a character in a book.

He picked up the phone.

'Are you ready?' a voice said.

It was Holt.

'For what?' asked Danny.

'Sightseeing.'

'I thought you had to work,' Danny said.

'I'm done,' Holt said. 'So are you ready?'

*

They took a taxi across the city. The hotel was in a built-up area, all office blocks. The taxi moved slowly through the packed streets. At times there were six lanes of traffic going each way.

Holt and Danny said nothing to each other until the car drew up at the foot of a large square on the other side of the river.

Holt paid the driver and Danny joined him on the pavement.

And there – above them – was a massive cathedral. Or was it a mosque? Danny wasn't sure. It was huge. Several swirling domes that looked like ice creams. All red and white and green. Not like the parish church Danny had to walk past on his way to and from school.

Then Danny saw Holt staring to his left. Across the square at a towering red wall. A city of yellow buildings behind it. A giant clock tower.

'What's that?' Danny asked.

'The Kremlin.'

'Really?' Danny stared.

This was where the president of Russia lived and worked. One of the most powerful men in the world. And where the leaders of Russia from the past, that he'd read about in his dad's books, had done their stuff.

They stood in the oversized square. Millions of

cobbles gently curving like a football pitch to huge buildings at either side.

'Then this is Red Square?' Danny said.

'Yep.'

They gazed around them. Everything was so big. The walls. The buildings. The square. Danny felt tiny. Like he was an ant. It made him feel edgy.

And he couldn't stop looking at the cathedral. He was used to churches that were small and one colour. This one was crazy.

'What do you think of the cathedral?' Danny asked. He wanted to see what Holt thought of it.

'It's St Basil's.'

'Right,' Danny said. 'But what do you think of it?'

Danny didn't want to say he thought it was ugly. But part of him thought that. From this side you could see six of the swirling domes, each brightly painted in different colours.

'I . . .' Holt paused. 'It's very impressive.'

'It's horrible,' Danny said.

'You reckon?'

'I do. It's too fancy.'

'It's one of the most famous landmarks in the world,' Holt said. 'It's just different.'

'Right,' said Danny. 'I'm just saying what I think.'

'Listen to this.' Holt had his guidebook out now. 'It was built by Ivan the Terrible. You've heard of him?'

'Yeah.'

'And he blinded the architect who made it because he didn't want him to make anything so beautiful again.'

'You sure he didn't blind him *before* he built it?' Danny muttered.

Holt smiled. 'And Napoleon – when he invaded – was going to blow it up. He filled it with gunpowder and set the fuses. But a miraculous rain shower put out the fires.'

'Oh well,' said Danny, shrugging. 'Nice try.'

'Jesus, Danny. You're so down on it. It's not *that* bad.'

'I suppose.'

'I bet there's loads of good stories about it,' Holt said. 'Most cathedrals act as a place of sanctuary – where people can hide if they're in trouble with the law. I bet a cathedral sees some interesting things go on in a country like this.'

Danny nodded. He was watching a line of soldiers walking towards them. All in long green coats and fur hats.

One at the front was dressed differently. He had on one of the massive brimmed hats. And a camouflage jacket, rather than a long coat.

The soldier – or was he a policeman? – gave Danny a hard stare.

'I reckon it'd be worth hiding from someone like him,' Holt said.

Danny nodded. He wanted to make a move. Out of this square that was making him feel more and more uneasy.

# SECRET AGENTS

The lobby of the President Hotel was fancy. Seriously fancy. Danny knew why the FA had chosen it for the England squad to stay in.

This was as good as a hotel could get. Dozens of tables and comfortable chairs were set out on a plush red carpet. Overhead, tens of thousands of tiny lights glittered white and gold. There was a balcony above, leaves and flowers cascading down.

He was sitting in an oversized armchair, trying to read *The Spy Who Came in from the Cold*. But he was mostly watching people come through the revolving doors, past two men in black suits with ties.

Security, Danny assumed.

In Danny's book, the character he'd thought was good had turned out to be a traitor. And the character he'd thought was a baddy was the nicest character of all. He was seriously confused.

In armchairs around the hotel lobby several groups of people were talking. Others were sitting alone. Reading newspapers. Stirring sugar into their drinks.

When people came into the hotel, most of them just stopped and stared. At the waterfall of light suspended over the lobby. At the spectacular plants cascading from the balcony. At the impressive reception desk, where four smartly dressed receptionists beamed smiles at the hotel's guests.

Others walked straight past the spectacular entrance to the set of four lifts without even glancing at the foyer. *They've been here before*, Danny thought. Used to it. As if this was a normal kind of place to be in, a place you could *ever* get used to.

Every few minutes Danny saw an England official. You could tell by the dark blue suit and FA badge they wore. Without exception. Most of them were quite old too. They looked unapproachable. Too important. Posh. Something like that.

But Danny was off limits anyway. Anton had told him: don't talk to anyone from the FA. And especially not the players. The press – and Holt included Danny in that – were not allowed to talk to the players. Not without an FA press officer there.

Danny was feeling a bit flat after the trip round Moscow with Anton. It'd been fun. Seeing the sights. Hearing about the cathedral. There was something about Anton telling him interesting facts that was a lot easier to bear than his mum or his dad doing it.

He'd wanted to know more.

But halfway through the tour, Holt took a call on his mobile – and had taxied Danny straight back to the hotel. He said he had to go and do an interview. With a footballer. But he couldn't say who. Danny could tell he wasn't telling the whole truth. So he asked if he could come too. But Holt had said no. Too quickly. Treating him like a kid again, Danny felt.

And now Danny was sitting in the hotel lobby, feeling left out. Still that sense that there was something funny going on.

Where did Holt have to go?

Why so suddenly?

Who had called him?

And what was so secret that Danny wasn't allowed to go along too? He'd thought Holt was going to take him everywhere on this trip. It wasn't like he didn't know how to behave around footballers.

Danny sat back in his seat. He was well aware that his week was getting stranger and stranger. First he witnessed what he was convinced was a murder attempt on an England goalkeeper. Then he was invited to Moscow for a World Cup qualifier as part of his school work experience. Now he was waiting for a journalist to return from a trip that Danny wasn't convinced he was telling the truth about.

For a moment a cloud passed through Danny's mind again. Holt. Was he being straight? Was he somehow involved in all this weirdness?

Then he told himself to shut up. He had to stop

thinking like this. There was no way Holt would be messed up in something dodgy. Anton was the most straightforward man he knew. And hadn't he supported Danny in the past?

Three kilometres away in another opulent hotel lobby, Anton Holt was sitting alone.

*He* was looking at people too. But not just any people. He was waiting for certain individuals in particular.

Most of the tables in this foyer were taken up by groups of men. No women. Many of the men were leaning forward, talking. Some in loud voices, attracting attention. Others in quiet voices, keeping their conversations to themselves.

Holt scanned each table.

The people he was looking for were not here.

But after waiting over an hour he saw a familiar figure. Tall. Thinner than he'd seen him before. With dark, not silver, hair. A deep tan. And dressed in a very expensive suit.

It was *him*. Holt knew it instinctively.

Although Holt had worked for weeks on the premise that this man was still alive, it was still a shock to see him. It was a man he knew well. A man he'd crossed swords with before. And he was sitting in a hotel that Holt had discovered, after much research, belonged to none other than Dmitri Tupolev, the Russian oligarch. That was what had brought the journalist here: knowing who owned the hotel and thinking that owner might be in league with an old friend.

And now that Holt could see that this man was alive and well, he knew that his theory could be true. That the Englishman and Tupolev were in talks: talks to plan the take-over of City FC and pitch the club into years of scandal and dodgy dealings.

Now he could write the story. The story of Sir Richard Gawthorpe's return.

Danny was getting bored in the England team hotel. No players to watch. No Holt. Told to wait here like a good little boy.

But now he'd been sitting for more than two hours, some of the things he was looking at had begun to stand out.

He remembered reading a thriller to his dad once. *12:23* by Eoin McNamee. It was all about surveillance. The book described a group of agents watching a famous couple who were visiting Paris. And the thing that had really stuck with Danny was that the agents didn't watch their targets for a few minutes, see what they needed to, then go home for their tea. They watched them for hours. Days. Weeks even. And that they weren't looking for dramatic behaviour or sudden moves. They were looking for patterns. Things that stood out: but that *didn't* stand out immediately. Things that only appeared obvious when you recognized the patterns of people's behaviour over a long time.

And that was what was happening to Danny.

There were two men in the lobby. Like Danny, they had been sitting in the lobby for over two hours. And had done nothing but read newspapers. Except they were both reading the same newspaper over and over again. The same page for ten minutes, then another ten minutes an hour later. And – although they sat opposite each other – neither had looked at the other once.

Three things that didn't sit right.

Who would re-read a newspaper when they were surrounded by the free magazines that were also on the hotel tables?

Who would sit waiting for two hours in the same place, directly opposite someone, without looking at them?

And why were they drinking carrot juice?

Danny immediately suspected who these men were. Agents. Russian agents. KGB – or whatever they were called now. FSB? He was convinced.

He slipped his phone out, and – pretending that he was looking at a text – he filmed the men and sent it to Charlotte with a short message:

**Secret agents. Prob KGB? Interesting? D x**

He understood who the men were, but what he *didn't* understand was: what were they doing in a hotel that was hosting the English first-team squad three days before the crunch Russia–England World Cup qualifying game?

Danny felt glad he'd filmed them.

# MONDAY

## HOMESICK

Danny woke at 2 a.m., Moscow time.

He opened the heavy hotel curtains to reveal his room's massive window and a panoramic view of Moscow, shrouded in darkness.

The city looked calm at night. There was a faint mist over the higher buildings that reminded Danny of home. Danny gazed at Moscow. Three buildings stood out. All three or four kilometres away. All tall. All looking like something out of a science fiction film – and lit up red.

Holt had told him about these buildings yesterday. They were called the Seven Sisters. Stalin – Russia's most brutal leader – had built them as government buildings. The Ministry for Foreign Affairs and six others. All seven were made to look scary. The reason: to make sure people in Soviet Moscow would behave themselves.

Danny turned round and looked at his bed, the TV and the rest of his room. It was posh. Seriously posh. He wasn't used to hotel rooms anyway, but this one was way over the top.

He felt out of sorts. Something wrong. If it hadn't been 2 a.m. he would have called his dad.

One thing that hadn't helped was that during the night he'd heard voices passing his door. Americans. Russians. French, maybe. The voices had made him feel uneasy. And the thought of going down into the hotel to have breakfast was worrying him. He wished he was at home. In his own room. So he could walk out of it and down the stairs to have a cup of tea with his dad before his mum and sister got up. Not among the hundreds of businessmen he had seen walking meaningfully down the corridors of this hotel as if they'd never had a moment's doubt in their lives.

Then it occurred to Danny that Moscow was three hours ahead of the UK. So it would be 11 p.m. at home. Not 2 a.m. His dad would still be downstairs, making a drink for his mum before they went to bed. If he called now he could talk to Dad. Maybe Mum.

Danny grabbed his phone and dialled the code: 00 44. Then his home number, minus the zero at the beginning.

At first there was no sound. Then a loud click. Then a muffled ringing tone that was nothing like the ringing tone of the phone at home. He worried he'd called the wrong number. *And* that someone might be listening in.

'Yeah?'

It was Emily.

'Hello, Emily,' Danny said.

'Danny!'

It was weird. Emily had said his name like she was pleased to hear him. Danny was thrown and didn't know what to say.

'Danny?' Emily repeated.

'Hello,' Danny said. 'How's it going?'

'OK,' Emily said. Her voice was a bit more guarded now.

'How are Mum and Dad?'

'Fine. What about Moscow? Is it rubbish?'

'It's great,' Danny said. He felt like telling Emily that he felt a bit weird. And that maybe it was a *bit* rubbish. But he knew she'd jump on it: use it to get one over on him.

There was a silence. Then Emily piped up, 'Have you passed on my good wishes to the Russian players? For the game.'

Danny grinned. This was more like it. Emily as he knew her.

'Yeah,' he replied. 'They said you're banned from Russia – for being a traitor to your own country.'

Emily said nothing.

'Is Dad there?' Danny asked.

'Yeah.'

'Can I talk to him? It's two pounds a minute.'

'Sorry!' Emily sounded cross.

'Nice though it is to talk to you,' Danny added. Meaning it.

'Yeah right,' Emily said. And the line went quiet.

Danny looked outside again. Suddenly the sky was alight with huge snowflakes. It was thrilling. Danny felt like he did at Christmas.

'Danny?' It was Dad. 'How's it going?'

'Great,' Danny said automatically. It was good to hear his dad's voice. He had a sudden sense that he missed his dad. Deeply.

'What have you seen?'

'Red Square. St Basil's. The Kremlin.' Danny reeled off a list of places. 'And snow. It's just started snowing.'

'Red Square?' Dad said, ignoring Danny's reference to snow. 'I've always wanted to go there.'

'It's just big, Dad. Everything's big. Even the snowflakes.'

Dad paused. 'Are you OK? You don't sound that happy.'

Danny frowned. 'It's all right,' he said. 'I'm just a bit . . . I don't know.'

'That's normal,' Dad said. 'You're bound to feel that. It's being away from home. But don't let it stop you having a good time and seeing some things. Just accept you'll feel weird. It's a part of the fun of travelling.'

Danny paused, then nodded to himself. 'OK,' he said.

'Is Anton looking after you?' Dad asked.

'Yeah. He's been good. He has to work too. But he took me out for a tour.'

'And did you start the book?'

Danny nodded again. 'It's great. But it's making me think everyone's a double agent. Everyone!'

Dad chuckled. 'Even Anton?'

'Yeah,' Danny said. 'Do you think . . . ?'

'Yeah, I'd watch him,' Dad said.

Danny laughed. Then he said, 'I'd better go. Is Mum there?'

'She's gone to bed already. Fast asleep.'

'I'll call later, then,' Danny promised.

He put his mobile down. The call had cost him over six quid. But it was worth it.

He lay back on the massive double bed. What now?

He could go out for a walk. See what Moscow was like at this time of the morning. Learn a few words of Russian. Or he could watch BBC News 24.

He decided on the Russian. He leaned back on his pillow and looked at the guide to Moscow Anton had given him. All the journalists had one: how to speak basic Russian words, how to call a taxi, how to use the underground.

No was *nyet* – нет.

Yes, *da* – да.

Thank you, *spasiba* – спасибо.

There were lots of words to do with football.

Stadium was *stadion* – стадион.

Football manager was *footbalniy myenyejyer* – футбалный менеджер.

Autograph was *avtograf* – автограф.

Danny read the words, then said them aloud. He wanted to be able to use some of them. He thought it was polite to be able to say thank you, at least.

After a few minutes Danny felt tired. He put his guide down and set his alarm for 6 a.m. He'd have a walk then.

He fell asleep quickly.

## THE INVITATION

Danny got back to the hotel from his walk and went to breakfast on his own. He stood near the entrance to the restaurant. He hoped other guests would think he was waiting for someone.

He'd enjoyed being out in the city before 7 a.m. Watching people going to work. Struggle in the snow. Buy newspapers. Park their cars. Argue with each other. Normal lives; not the touristy things that always looked staged. Normal life was always more interesting.

And the snow was beautiful, smoothing the hard edges and high buildings that Danny had objected to. He felt excited. Like a kid going sledging. He remembered doing it with his dad before he was blind.

Danny had spent a bit of time watching a pair of policemen. To see how they worked. What they were like. Then they'd spotted him and moved to come over to him. So he'd left – and returned to the hotel.

But hotels freaked Danny out. He wasn't really sure what he was meant to do at the best of times. But now? Should he stay near the restaurant entrance to be seated? Or sit down and wait to be brought food? Or help himself to the tables of fruit and cereal and meats?

Standing there, confused, he felt a hand on his shoulder. He jumped.

'Danny.'

It was Holt.

'I'm sorry about last night,' Holt said. 'I got tied up.'

Danny nodded. He still felt left out, but he wasn't going to throw a strop. He knew Holt had pulled a lot of strings to get him to Moscow.

'It's OK,' Danny said. 'It's your job.'

'Anyway,' Holt nodded. 'I've got some news.'

'Yeah?'

'We all had a press release slipped under our doors this morning.'

'Who?'

'The media. There's going to be a massive reception tonight for the press, the players and the FA. At this rich guy's country estate. And we're all invited.'

Danny assumed Holt meant he could go too, but he didn't want to push it.

'You're coming,' Holt said, reading his mind. Then he stopped himself. 'I mean, would you like to come, Danny?'

That evening two coaches arrived – both silver with black-tinted glass. They were accompanied by four large black people-carriers. All with tinted windows too. And what looked like a police light on top.

Although there were a few centimetres of snow on the streets, there was none in the hotel grounds. It was as if it was too posh to be affected by the weather.

It was bitter outside. Danny felt the skin on his face was beginning to freeze.

He went over to have a look at one of the people-carriers, but Holt pulled him back.

'Watch it,' Holt warned.

'Why?'

'Just be easy round these guys.' Holt nodded at a pair of men eyeing them. Short cropped hair. Huge muscles. Tight black T-shirts. Scruffy jackets. Stubble. Pistols stuffed down their trousers.

Danny stepped back. 'Who are they?'

'Tupolev's private army,' Holt answered.

'Who?'

'Tupolev. The guy who's putting on the reception. He's a . . . an oligarch.'

'Like Abramovich?'

'Yeah, but richer.'

'Richer than Abramovich?'

'Oh yes.'

'Why does he need a private army?'

'Status,' Holt said. 'They all have one. Makes them look hard. And cool. And – I suppose – to genuinely protect them. There's plenty of people who'd like a piece of Tupolev's action.'

'How come you know so much about it?' Danny asked.

Holt shrugged.

Danny and Holt got on the coach. A few of the other journalists nodded to Danny. They were friendly with him. Even though he wasn't one of them.

'So how did he get his money? This Tupolev?' Danny asked, once they'd sat down; Danny had headed for the back of the bus like he always did on school trips. He remembered reading about a rich Russian: *his* name had begun with T. Was it him?

'Don't ask,' Holt said.

'Why not?'

'I'll tell you later.' Holt was making gestures. Putting his finger over his lips, shaking his head. Then tapping his ear.

'What?' Danny said.

Holt shook his head again.

'Shall I shut up?' Danny said.

Holt nodded. 'Let's talk when we're off this coach Dmitri Tupolev has kindly put on for us.'

They drove first through Moscow. Along the enormous highway that cut through the city. Huge grey buildings either side of them. Then massive parks. Spectacular churches. Spindly tram wires overhead. Snow piled in heaps at the side of the road.

But the coach was warm. Its heating on full blast. Danny soon forgot it was freezing outside. Minus ten.

The traffic was heavy – and endless. Filthy grey and white cars stopping and starting as they edged over the river. The only features standing out were the red walls of the Kremlin and the enormous statue of a bearded man languishing on the steps of a large oblong building. White shading his left side.

'That's Dostoevsky,' Holt said.

'Who?'

'He wrote *Crime and Punishment*. A novel. The first detective novel,' Holt explained. 'A man kills two old women with an axe and tries to work out why he did it. You should read it. It's a laugh.'

Danny made a mental note. He would.

Once they were out of the centre, the coach picked up speed. First they saw miles and miles of apartment blocks. Twenty storeys high, like blocks of flats at home; but each block the width of ten English blocks of flats.

'Most people in Moscow live in blocks like that,' Holt said.

'Right,' Danny murmured. He was glad he lived in a terrace back home.

As they were talking a message came in on his phone. He checked it.

**No. Still boring. More pls. C xx**

Danny winced. He knew Charlotte was joking, but it was important to him that she was impressed. He needed something more.

Once they'd passed the apartment blocks, the scenery opened out to a white featureless land. And after that endless trees, thin silvery trunks covered in snow.

'Those trees go on for hundreds of miles,' Holt said. 'That's it after Moscow.'

After another half-hour the coaches, still tailed by the black people-carriers, turned off on to a smaller road, then one smaller still. The atmosphere in the coach had been chatty and excitable for the trip so far, but once they were on the minor road, Danny noticed a quiet descend over the coach.

'We're nearly there, I think,' Holt said. 'Look. That'll be it.'

Danny looked.

The house they were approaching was huge. He thought they were going to someone's country cottage. But this was more like the stately home he saw on the hills every time his mum drove them along the M1. It looked like a castle. And had dozens of chimneys. There must have been over a hundred rooms, easy.

'Does someone actually live here?'

Holt nodded.

The coaches drove slowly through open fields. Danny noticed a small group of deer feeding in a dip. Then more groups of deer. There were actually hundreds.

Holt was staring at a lake, a massive lake, hundreds of wild birds suddenly lifting from its surface.

'This is amazing,' Danny said. 'Are we going in there?'

'Oh yes.'

'Is it going to be posh?' Danny asked, looking down at his jeans and T-shirt.

'It is.'

Danny nodded. He hated posh. Normally.

But just this once he thought it'd be interesting to see what this sort of posh was really like. It was the chance of a lifetime.

# A DIFFERENT KIND OF PARTY

This was not the kind of party Danny was used to. Nothing like the one he had been to two days earlier in England. There were no champagne fountains there. No waiters dressed head to foot in white. No skinned, dead animal being roasted over an open fire.

And – added to that – Danny could not get his head round the fact that he was standing with the England football team in a huge room with a ceiling painted with figures and animals. A room that was more like a church than a house. It felt like a dream. That was the only way Danny could find to describe to himself how he felt.

He stood back from the crowd and began to film. *This* would impress Charlotte. He made sure he got in a couple of players. Ones even Charlotte would recognize. Peter Day. She'd know him. Tall. Always smiling. Everybody liked Peter Day.

The more Danny looked, the more amazing the room seemed.

Long gold curtains hung from the ceiling, draped across the room like the sails of ships.

A table over thirty metres long offered hundreds of

dishes. Fish. Meats. Vegetables. And dozens of small pastry shapes.

As well as champagne, you could drink any one of hundreds of selections at the bar. Beers. Wines. Spirits. Cocktails.

Danny stopped filming and asked the waitress if she could find him a Coke. She was not much older than he was. She smiled.

'I try,' she said.

She came back two minutes later with a glass of Coke on a silver tray.

'*Spasiba*,' Danny said.

The waitress smiled again, then left Danny to gaze around the room.

There were statues of bulls and people banging tambourines. Some of them naked. And oil paintings of people eating grapes. It was a strange place. A very strange place.

Danny finished his film, turned his back and sent it off to Charlotte.

Five minutes later a man got up to speak on a platform at the front of the hall. His audience turned to stare at him immediately.

Danny noticed a pair of men watching the people as the man stood, their hands clasped together at the front, wires coiling down from their ears into their shirts. They wore matching suits.

This was clearly the man who'd put the reception on. One of the richest men in the world. *This* was Dmitri Tupolev, the Russian oligarch.

'Ladies and gentlemen,' the man said in what seemed like perfect English to Danny. 'I welcome you humbly to my home.'

He was about fifty years old. But he could have passed for forty. He was tall and fit. His skin was bronzed. His hair black. And his clothes – a suit and a pink tie – were so smart Danny assumed they must have been made to fit him. He wondered if he was one of those rich people he'd heard about who only ever wore clothes once before replacing them.

Danny observed as the men in suits began to applaud. The applause spread – and continued for a minute. Danny felt obliged to join in, as did Holt. It was like some cheesy game show. The suits warming the audience up.

'We come together two days before my beloved Russia are playing your England football team for a place in the World Cup finals,' Tupolev said, once the applause had died down. 'It will be a fair game, of course.'

Danny frowned. That was a strange thing to say. Why would he say that? Weren't all games fair?

Tupolev continued. 'I wish to welcome your England team players, the Football Association and the ladies and gentlemen of the English mass media. You are all welcome to enjoy the delights we have on offer here.'

Danny was already becoming bored by the speech. Why didn't he just get to the point? Blah, blah, blah . . .

As the man went on – speaking, but saying nothing that meant anything – Danny wondered if the game *would* be fair. What had Tupolev meant? Why would you say that? No one ever said that. It was just a given. And his mind started running away with itself, like it always did.

*Maybe this reception was a ruse*, Danny thought. *To get all the England players together and drug or poison them. So Russia could win.* Danny watched England players tucking into plates laden with the food that had been offered to them. Danny had heard that the England team took their own food when they were playing away. Even their own cooks.

And then Danny noticed Matt McGee.

McGee stood out because he was the only person not looking at Tupolev making his boring speech. Apart from Danny. In fact, McGee was watching the door at the side of the hall. Danny moved back a few paces so he could see more. And he was shocked to see McGee suddenly leaving.

Moments later, McGee was followed by the two men in suits who had started the applause earlier.

Danny made to go after them. Instinctively. Just to

see what was happening. Why was it that England goalkeepers were always so interesting?

But suddenly he felt Holt pull him back.

'Stick close to me,' the reporter whispered.

Danny had forgotten Holt was even there. 'I'm just going –' he began.

'Where?'

'For a look round.'

'Danny. Please, please stay close to me. This is a nice party. All very friendly. But don't go snooping around. I know you. There's nothing to see here. Nothing. You've seen his henchmen? The guys in suits? Please don't cross them.'

'I need to go to the loo,' Danny said.

'The loo's that way.' Holt pointed up the wide staircase that – like in the hotel foyer – swept up a wall on one side of the room.

'Can I go, then?' Danny asked in a truculent voice.

Holt eyed him, then nodded.

Danny climbed the stairs, skirted a corridor and headed left into the toilets. Amazing toilets. Polished wooden fittings. Huge mirrors. Soap and cream dispensers. A pile of flannels that Danny assumed were to dry your hands on.

But surrounded by all this luxury, Danny couldn't get Holt out of his mind. He was sounding more and more like his mum. *Don't do that! Do this! Don't go here!* Danny had thought it would be fun with Holt because he was younger than his parents. Closer to his own age, in fact. But he was still a bossy adult.

Danny didn't really need the toilet, but Holt might be looking out for him if he went back to the main hall. Then he noticed the windows that ran along the top of the cubicles. Making sure that there was no one else around, Danny went into a cubicle, stood on the toilet seat and looked out of the window. He saw a large courtyard and a pitch-black sky filled with stars. And there, in the courtyard, he saw Matt McGee.

McGee was leaning against a doorway. Danny saw him exhale upwards, his breath like smoke coming out of his lungs on the cold night. But it couldn't be smoke: no footballer would be stupid enough to smoke.

Then McGee looked at his watch. As he did, the two men in suits that Danny had seen in the main hall stood either side of him. Danny could tell who was talking from the vapour trails their breath left. The smaller of the men in black did most of the talking, with McGee sometimes chipping in. Danny tried to catch the expression on McGee's face, to see what was going on. But all he could see was McGee nodding.

Eventually the conversation between the men in black and Matt McGee came to an end, and then – it seemed to Danny – the three men just stood in silence for at least ten seconds.

Then the smaller man stuck out his hand. For a moment McGee did not extend his: but then he did, shaking hands.

England's keeper shaking hands with one of Tupolev's private army: what was going on?

Now Danny had serious doubts about McGee. Although he'd met him and thought him nice, although he'd heard Alex Finn vouch for him, there was no plausible explanation for his talking to men from Dmitri Tupolev's private army.

Danny needed to get to Holt. Holt knew things. So did Danny. They had to share their ideas. And fast.

## GOING SOLO

'Anton. Come on.'

Danny grabbed Holt's arm and tried to pull him across the hall.

The speech was over. Tupolev had disappeared. Holt stopped and stared at Danny crossly. 'What is it?'

Most of the guests were chatting and eating. Four musicians were playing gentle music.

'McGee,' Danny whispered. 'He's talking to these men outside. The ones in suits. I'm not sure what's going on.'

Holt put his hand up. He looked like a teacher trying to silence a room.

Danny tried not to feel angry.

'Danny. Stop this.' Holt was talking in a low voice. 'You're running around looking for trouble. There's no story here. Just leave it.'

Danny looked straight into Holt's eyes. And, just as he thought he would, Holt looked away. Now Danny wanted to challenge the journalist. Say he knew there was something going on and that he wasn't sure whose side Holt was on. But he didn't know how to put it. How do you say something like that?

'Danny,' Holt said firmly, 'your mum and dad put you in my care. Like it or not, you're fourteen, and legally a child, and I'm the adult who's been put in charge of you. I have to look out for you. If I let you go after a pair of armed men . . . well, it's ridiculous.'

Danny nodded. He knew this was all true. 'B-but –' he stammered.

'No buts, Danny.'

'Let's just go and look. See what's going on. The men he was talking to are the ones from the black people-carriers. You know: the ones with guns.'

'*I'll* look,' Holt said. 'Will that satisfy you?'

Danny shook his head.

'It's either me or neither of us,' Holt said.

Danny frowned, then nodded. 'And what do I do?' he asked.

'Get another Coke. Look at the statues.'

'Great,' Danny said. 'Statues.'

'So, I'm going?' Holt asked, ignoring his remark.

Danny nodded. 'But you have to tell me everything.'

'Sure,' Holt said. And he was off. Moving quickly to the same door McGee had left a few minutes before – and had yet to emerge from.

And Danny wondered why Holt was so quick across the room if he was convinced nothing was going on.

*

Above the hall there was a balcony where you could stand and watch everyone eating and drinking and talking. In the past it had been where the Russian secret police, the KGB, had watched people they thought were spying on Russia. But today an Englishman was standing there, watching. The Englishman Holt had seen in the hotel that belonged to Dmitri Tupolev.

Sir Richard Gawthorpe. Also known as Kenneth Francis.

Sir Richard's face looked alert, a blush across his cheeks. He knew he could not attend the party. But Tupolev had given him a room on the balcony, so he could watch from above, so he could see the England players, the FA officials, some of whom he knew well. And he had been enjoying watching them – reliving old times – until he had spotted a smaller figure.

A boy.

He had to look three times to be sure he had seen who he thought he'd seen.

If anyone had been looking at him, they would have seen that Sir Richard's face looked shocked at first. But then they'd have seen it break into a smile. A maniacal beaming smile.

He had seen the boy who had forced him to give up his old identity. The boy who had taken on Sir Richard Gawthorpe and won.

Now he had a chance: for revenge.

*

Danny kept his eyes on the door until he spotted Holt coming back into the hall. He tried to read his face as Holt approached, but Holt was neither smiling nor frowning.

'Well?'

'They're just talking, Danny. One of them speaks English.'

'That's it?'

'Yeah. I listened. They're talking. About football, would you believe it?'

Danny wanted to argue with Holt. But there was no point. This was going nowhere. Holt knew things but wouldn't tell Danny. Now what Danny had to do was get away from Holt. Do some finding out for himself.

And Holt gave him the opportunity within seconds.

'I have to set up some interviews for tomorrow's edition,' Holt said. 'Can you stay here? And not move?'

'Sure,' Danny said, trying not to sound too keen.

'I'll not be long. I just have to arrange times. That's all. Don't wander off.'

'Yeah,' said Danny. 'I'll have some food.'

When Holt had gone, Danny checked around the room to make sure no one was watching. Then he slipped out of the door he'd seen McGee and Holt go through.

## THE CHASE

Outside it was dark. Now that the sun had gone down it felt even colder. Very cold. He could feel the air stinging his face.

Danny stood in the doorway to the courtyard where he'd seen McGee and the men in suits. There was no sign of them now. And yet none of them had come back into the reception.

The courtyard was empty.

Danny looked around, trying to take everything in. And he listened. He was as likely to hear people as see them.

It was quite a courtyard. Huge wooden doors on each of the four walled sides. Like the doors of a castle or a palace, studded with black metal. A slate roof. Cobbles on the ground. Through one of the doors – half open – Danny saw a row of cars. He went to have a closer look, to find it was a vast garage. He recognized a Ferrari. A Rolls-Royce. A Porsche. And another extreme sports car he remembered seeing on *Top Gear*. The man who owned this place certainly was loaded.

The garage smelled of oil and petrol fumes. But it was clean. Each car looking like it was polished daily.

As Danny entered the garage, he heard voices. Coming from the back.

Danny breathed in and took slow, quiet steps.

They were definitely English voices. One was a northern English voice. McGee. Unmistakably McGee. The other voice was Russian, but talking good English.

Danny ducked down and moved slowly to the first car. The Ferrari. He peeped over the top of it. He felt terrified. The sense that he could be caught. But he needed to know what was going on. He used that need to overcome his fear.

There were four men.

The two men in suits stood at a distance now from the pair who were talking. McGee and – Danny couldn't quite believe it – Dmitri Tupolev. The man who'd made the speech.

What was Matt McGee doing talking to the Russian billionaire? And hidden away from all the other guests.

This was definitely not right.

Maybe Tupolev was tapping McGee up. That was what they called it. Trying to get him to sign for the Russian champions. To leave England.

Danny acted quickly. He didn't need to weigh this one up. He got out his mobile phone, activated the video and held it just over the roof of the Ferrari. He squatted so as not to be seen and watched the scene through the mirror of the car, hoping he was pointing his camera at the people – and not just the roof.

The annoying thing was, he couldn't hear what they were saying. All he could see was McGee nodding, then holding his hands up. The Russian made no gestures. He was just staring at McGee as he spoke.

Danny hoped his phone would pick up what was being said.

Then, suddenly, without any warning, the four men were walking towards Danny.

Danny had seen or heard no cues that this was about to happen. One minute they were talking, the next coming between the cars towards him.

Danny tucked his phone away and tried to roll under the Ferrari. But, of course, there was no room under the low-slung car. He felt panic rising in him and tried to calm himself down, tried to breathe deep and long. But it's hard to keep a grip on your mind when you feel your life could be in danger.

He edged round the Ferrari and hid under the Rolls-Royce, just as eight feet came marching past him.

Danny held his breath. He didn't dare breathe out or in. All the things Holt had said to him about Tupolev and how Danny should be really careful flooded his mind. Maybe he really *was* in danger. Why did he *always* get himself into situations like this?

Then the feet stopped. Right next to Danny. If he

had wanted to, Danny could have reached out and touched the shoes that were closest to him. The strangest pair of shoes he'd ever seen. It was like they had scales. Danny wondered what they were made of. Snake skin? Or crocodile?

Danny took out his phone and began to film again, his hands trembling with fear.

The scaly shoes were facing the straightforward black shiny leather of McGee's own.

This time Danny heard the voices loud and clear.

'A penalty in the first half. A misjudged cross in the second. Yes?'

That was the Russian accent. Tupolev. No question.

There was no reply.

'Yes?' said Tupolev, louder, his voice making Danny shudder.

Danny saw the black shoes cross each other, like the other man was adjusting his footing.

'I heard what you said,' a voice replied. McGee's.

Danny exhaled. He couldn't help himself.

There was a long silence during which none of the feet moved.

'OK,' Tupolev said.

The black shoes uncrossed themselves. Then all eight feet moved noisily back into the courtyard.

Danny lay under the Rolls-Royce for a minute. He'd give the men time to leave before he emerged.

And anyway, he had a lot to think about.

What had he just overheard? A Russian billionaire asking an England goalkeeper to let in two goals?

What was going on?

He had to tell Holt. Everything.

But first he wanted to send the film he'd just made to Charlotte. Just in case he lost his phone. Or had it taken off him. This would satisfy her, surely. There was no way she could say *this* was boring.

He quickly texted Charlotte.

**Look after this. Show no one. D x**

Then he slid from under the Rolls-Royce, brushed himself down and began to head back across the courtyard to the buzz of voices coming from the reception.

'*Èj!*' Danny heard a shout.

It seemed to have come from above. Danny didn't have a clue what had been said. But he knew he had to get away.

Instead of going back into the main hall, where he could easily bump into Tupolev or some of his men in suits, Danny darted towards a gateway at the far end of the courtyard. Out into the open.

Behind him he heard pounding footsteps. Just one pair of feet, he reckoned.

He took a quick look.

One man. In black. Gaining on Danny.

Danny sprinted round the side of what looked, in the dark, like a horse-drawn carriage. There was a pile of earth on the floor. Danny hurdled it, and realized it wasn't earth, but a massive heap of horse manure. It stank. Danny ran on, looking for an escape route.

He heard the man come after him. Too close. Ten metres behind him. Danny gagged. He was terrified. If this man got him, here on the edge of a forest, in the middle of the Russian countryside, he could do anything to Danny and no one would know.

Danny kicked on. And, as he did, he heard a scuffing and a short cry. The footsteps had stopped. Danny looked back. The man had fallen over. In the manure. He was covered in it.

Danny had gained a few seconds. But he had to use them wisely.

Where now? Back round the front of the house? Into the trees fifty metres away? Behind one of the parked-up coaches?

Danny chose the trees. He sprinted across the grass and darted behind the first tree he saw.

Fortunately there was no moonlight, so when the man had regained his footing, he could only look about himself, before running round the front of the house.

Danny stood still as he tried to regulate his breathing. In, out. In, out. Slowly. He felt sick. Being chased was terrifying. It threw his body into a panic. But now he had to calm down. Work things out. Quickly.

So what should he think now? He'd heard Matt McGee talking to the Russians about the match. McGee had appeared to agree to throwing the game. Although he'd not said he would exactly, it was the easiest conclusion to come to.

Danny's mind was in a whirl. Any detective would be thinking of McGee as the main suspect now. The man who was at the centre of some crime or scam. But Danny didn't want to believe it.

Then he realized: he didn't have to *believe* it. He just had to have it as a possibility. It didn't have to be true until it actually happened.

And that's what Danny resolved. He'd try and do something to make it *not* happen, try and stop people from fixing the game.

Danny decided to wait for ten minutes before he did anything. He'd just stand there. Then he'd go back to the party.

Five minutes later his phone buzzed. It was on silent. He always kept it on silent. Just in case. He looked at the screen. A text from Charlotte. His heart started pounding again. He opened her message. She'd have seen his films from the garage.

**What the hell is going on? Who is this? Text me now to say you are OK. C xxx**

Danny smiled – and texted Charlotte back:

**OK. D**

Then he stood at the edge of a Russian forest, thousands of miles away from home. And waited.

Five more minutes. Then he'd go back to the party.

## GOOD FRIEND

Danny had been standing in the woods without moving a muscle.

Although he could see no one looking for him, he knew they might be watching. That was why he'd chosen to wait – and to do nothing. That would be what they least expected.

As he waited, Danny listened to the sounds coming from the woods. Rustles. Screeches. And snaps. He smiled. They could rustle and screech and snap all they liked – he wasn't scared of wildlife tonight.

But he jumped when his phone started to buzz in his pocket. A call this time. Not a text.

A call? From who? Holt? Worrying where he was?

Danny looked at the screen, cupping his hands round it, so the light it gave off wouldn't be seen.

Charlotte.

Danny fumbled with the phone, nearly dropping it.

'Hello?' he whispered.

'What's going on? What the hell are you doing? Who were those men in the video?'

'It's some Russians ...' Danny tried to explain, keeping his voice quiet.

'I thought I told you to look after yourself. I've been worried. Are you safe?'

'I'm OK.'

'Then why are you *whispering*, Danny?'

Danny grinned. 'I'm hiding,' he said.

'What? Hiding? From who? Danny, tell me.'

'Some men. We're at some rich guy's house. At a party. I went for a look round and . . . well, just keep the film. Save it. It proves something.'

'What?'

'The taller man. He's the England keeper, Matt McGee. He's talking to the other man, Dmitri Tupolev. It might be evidence.'

'Evidence?'

'Please, just keep it. This call's costing two pounds a minute.'

'I don't care how much it costs. What I *do* care about is that you're safe.'

'I'm safe,' Danny said. Something made him smile.

'Are you sure?'

'I'm sure.'

'In that case,' Charlotte said, 'I've got news.'

'Yeah?' Danny wondered what she could have to say to him. The first thought that jumped into his head was that she was going to announce she had a boyfriend. The idea horrified him.

'That stuff you told me about McGee,' she went on. 'At the party.'

'Yeah?'

'About him knowing that guy. The criminal?'

'Yeah?'

'Well, I told the police. They didn't realize McGee and Barnes knew each other. They had no link. So they only went and raided Barnes's properties. They'd been looking for an excuse anyway. And guess what?'

'What?'

'They found the presses – for the counterfeit money – and loads of dodgy cash.'

Danny's heart began to thump. 'And the guy, Barnes?' he asked, hopeful.

'And him. They arrested him and some others.'

'Brilliant. But what about McGee? Did they say anything about him?'

'Not officially.'

Danny paused. 'But . . . unofficially.'

'Well, the officer who I gave the information to says one of the men they arrested has said something that clears McGee. Sort of.'

'Brilliant,' Danny said.

'Is it?'

'Yeah.'

'Why?'

'Because I want him to be clean.'

'So what's he up to with this Russian guy, then?' Charlotte asked. 'If he's so clean.'

'I'm not sure,' Danny said, as an owl hooted in the depths of the wood.

'But you think?'

'He could be taking a bribe to throw the game,' Danny said. 'It looks like that. But it's not true. I'm sure . . . well, almost sure.'

Charlotte said nothing for a moment. Then: 'Where are you, Danny?'

Danny knew she'd heard the owl hooting. 'In a wood,' he said.

'Why?'

'I'm hiding.'

'So you said. Who from?'

'A Russian billionaire's private army,' Danny replied.

Charlotte paused again.

'You said you were *safe*. Danny. I'm worried. I . . . care about you.'

Danny wanted to say the same thing back. He cared about Charlotte too. A lot.

'I'm safe,' he said. 'Trust me. I've not lied to you, have I?'

'No,' Charlotte said. 'But all this detective stuff you do. You need to be careful.'

'I am.'

'You'd better be. If you don't come home alive, I'll kill you.'

'OK,' Danny said, the grin still on his face long after Charlotte had put her phone down.

# *TUESDAY*

## *FOLLOWING McGEE*

Tuesday. The day before the big game.

Danny had breakfast with Holt. He decided to try some of the Russian food on offer today. Blini, which were long soft eggy cakes. And some small balls of jelly that looked like jam. Danny ate some of the blini. They were OK. Then he tried the jam. He nearly spat it out. It was really salty. Or fishy. He couldn't tell. He grabbed a cup of tea to take the taste away. Now he felt sick.

'I've got some more stuff to do this morning,' Holt said, eyeing him, but not mentioning the food. 'An interview with an official. But he wants me to go alone.'

'Don't worry,' Danny said. 'I reckon I'll do some sightseeing this morning.'

'I'll be free this afternoon,' Holt said, frowning. 'How about we check out some more places in the guidebook? Get some presents? Can you wait?'

Danny could still feel a tension between them from last night. But neither of them had acknowledged it.

'OK,' Danny said, smiling. He might get his mum and dad presents today. Maybe something for Paul and Charlotte. But there was no way Emily was getting a Russian doll.

'In fact, shall we go and have a look at the stadium later this afternoon?' Holt suggested. 'Try and get in to have a look round before it's overrun with security tomorrow?'

'Sounds good,' Danny said.

Danny had decided to be friendly with Holt. He didn't want to play the grumpy child any more. He knew Holt had a job to do. And, although he had big questions to ask about what Holt was up to, he knew now was not the time. One of his dad's favourite detectives was called Maigret. He'd always wait for the right moment to ask a question. Even though he'd known what to ask for hours, even days. That was what good detective work was about. Timing.

'How about I come back at midday?' Holt asked. 'We'll find somewhere to have lunch. Can you amuse yourself in the hotel until then?'

Danny nodded. He hoped he'd have his appetite back by then.

Lunchtime arrived and passed. Holt phoned at 1 p.m. to say he'd been delayed. Danny decided to be brave. He was on his own in a city where barely anyone spoke English. He could have sat in his room. Waited all day. But there was something he really wanted to see in Moscow.

Lenin's tomb.

He ordered a sandwich from room service and then went out into the city.

He didn't want to see Lenin's tomb because he was a big fan of Russian history. He knew Lenin had been the first leader of Russia after it'd had its revolution. But that was about it. The thing was, he'd read about Lenin's tomb in the guidebook. You could go in and see his *body*. His actual *dead* body. A body that had been dead for eighty-five years.

The body was in a building called a mausoleum. Something about that appealed to Danny. It was horrible. Really horrible. But he couldn't resist.

The guidebook had said that you could see his face and that his ears were all withered and tiny. Also, that loads of parts of his body had been replaced with wax and that some people thought Lenin was pretty much all wax now.

Gross.

Danny set off. The hotel was quite close to Red Square. According to the map he had to walk over the river, past a large cathedral with golden domes, take a right along the river and he'd be there.

Coming along and then across the river had been a struggle. The roads were so busy it'd been hard to find a place to cross.

But Danny made it eventually.

Red Square was still enormous. A huge ring of

concrete bollards surrounded the mausoleum. Groups of people gawped at the weird cathedral, the mausoleum, the Kremlin.

The walls that went along one side of the square were so big – and the square itself so big – that Danny felt tiny. There was something about the scale of the place that was wrong. It was like the people were being made to feel that small.

The mausoleum was a small red building that would have looked quite big if it had not been dwarfed by the walls of the Kremlin. It had the letters ЛЕНИН across it. Several people were having their photographs taken, grinning into the cameras with the building holding their dead former leader inside. Including young children.

Danny frowned. The place gave him the creeps.

But he still wanted to see the body.

He walked towards the entrance. There were two soldiers stood staring blankly out across the square. He thought about asking them if he could go in, but neither would meet his eyes.

He was getting nowhere. And beginning to lose his nerve.

And that was when he saw Matt McGee walk straight in front of him. Less than a hundred metres away. Across the front of the mausoleum. Towards the right of Red Square.

Where was *he* going? On his own in Moscow centre? Were footballers allowed to do that? Danny looked around him for some FA security people, expecting to see some. But there was no one obvious.

What was McGee doing? Maybe he was just sightseeing like Danny. Maybe he liked to get away from the claustrophobia of the hotel. Footballers could be into cathedrals and things like that. Maybe even mausoleums.

Danny knew what he had to do. Follow. That was the only way to get answers to his questions.

But he had to do it right.

How many times had he read about following people in crime novels? Tailing, it was called. There were several principles. He knew them by heart.

One: stay far back enough not to be seen, but not so far back as to lose your target.

Two: don't follow the target step by step. Try and cross roads so you're not just following in his footsteps directly.

Three: be ready to turn up a side road if you're spotted. But never do it as soon as your target sees you. It would be too obvious.

Danny waited. He let McGee get a hundred metres ahead of him, then he followed.

This was more interesting than looking at a body that had been dead for eighty-five years.

Definitely.

As soon as Danny set off across the square, a man began to follow *him*. Using the same techniques, he kept a hundred metres behind, talking rapid English into his mobile phone. The man watched Danny as he turned out of the square, then moved in behind him.

## THE ATTACK

Danny always stayed at least fifty metres behind McGee – in case his target looked back. Because, after all, McGee did know who Danny was. They'd spoken, briefly, outside the toilet on the plane. And been at the same party the night before.

But McGee did not look back. Sometimes he dawdled, moving suddenly slower. He was walking like a man following someone, not someone being followed himself. Danny looked ahead, but could see no one McGee might be following.

He got his phone out and set it to take a video, his finger over the record button. So he was ready.

Danny followed McGee past some sort of memorial, a flame burning at the foot of the Kremlin wall. It was guarded by three sullen sentries. All with fur hats. Danny had to find his way round several people standing staring at the flame. Then McGee went through an enormous queue of people. All waiting, Danny assumed, to get into the Kremlin. Danny took his time edging past the people. He didn't want to get too close to McGee. This crowd was the perfect cover.

But, next, they headed away from the crowds, down

the side of a major road, heavy traffic coming alongside them. If Danny needed to cross the road now, to avoid being seen, he would have had no chance. That tactic was not available to him. All he had was turning to walk the other way. And that would look really obvious. If McGee stopped, Danny would be stuffed.

But McGee was not stopping. He seemed to be heading back to the river. They'd walked around three sides of the Kremlin. Danny wondered where McGee was going. He could hardly be doing this for exercise. The air was so polluted and dirty that it was the last thing a sportsman should be doing the day before a big game. It'd be as bad as smoking.

Something had to happen soon. Danny could feel it. But what?

McGee approached a crossing. There was a policeman in the middle of the road. He'd stopped one stream of traffic – five lanes of it – just at the right time, holding up a black-and-white stick authoritatively, allowing McGee and a figure fifty metres ahead of him to cross. McGee sprinted across the road. But Danny held back. He had to. He couldn't just go after McGee. Not so soon. They'd be too close. So he waited. And that's why, when the policeman started the traffic again, Danny was left on one side of the busy road, McGee on the other.

Danny watched impatiently as McGee walked along

the side of the river, then down what he assumed were stone steps leading to the waterside.

Hundreds of cars had come past already. The traffic was endless. Danny was stranded.

Eventually the policeman stopped the traffic and waved at Danny to cross.

Danny walked sensibly until he was past the policeman. Then he ran across the rest of the road. In front of a large black people-carrier that skidded to a halt, missing him by metres. But Danny didn't have time to worry about that. He wanted to see what McGee was up to. Was it related to last night? This *had* to be more than a stroll around Moscow. McGee was walking in a circle – not actually going anywhere. Danny ran over a large expanse of grass, close to the river. Then to the steps he'd seen McGee disappear down.

He turned a corner and headed down.

And that was when he saw Matt McGee grappling with another man on the steps. Danny's finger hit the record button on his phone camera instinctively.

At first, Danny assumed *McGee* was being assaulted. He went down the steps and shouted, hoping that would stop whatever was happening. And he saw the other man stare up, distracted just like he wanted. But instead of the other man stopping what he was doing, maybe casting an angry glance at Danny, Danny saw a look of *horror* on his face.

Horror because he was falling.

Danny must have looked shocked too. Because he'd recognized the man McGee was fighting with. The falling man. It was Robert Skatie. England's other keeper.

What the hell was going on?

Skatie fell backwards, twisting in the air. He landed about six steps down, first on his shoulder, then rolling on to his back. Danny watched his head jerk backwards as he hit the steps.

And then Danny saw McGee staring at him, waving his arms, beckoning Danny.

Danny shook his head and turned to run back up the steps to find the traffic policeman. It was all he could think to do. But when he started up the stairs he saw four men.

One was the Englishman who had been following him. And, although he looked different physically, Danny recognized who it was.

For a moment he was stunned. Faced with the man he least wanted to see in the world, the man who had sent him to die in the bowels of City Stadium.

Sir Richard Gawthorpe.

The other three were dressed in black. He remembered what Anton had called them. Tupolev's private army.

'Run.'

The voice had come from right next to him. From McGee. Snapping Danny out of his confusion.

'Come on. Run!'

Danny felt McGee's hand on him, yanking him down the stairs. It felt like McGee had lifted him to the bottom of the steps.

'Go!' McGee snapped.

Danny looked up at McGee. McGee's face was crumpled.

But Danny couldn't move. He was paralysed with fear.

'GO!' McGee shouted in Danny's face, releasing him from his grip.

So Danny did. He had no option. He'd witnessed a fight between two of England's finest goalkeepers. He'd seen a private army coming down the steps, possibly to get him. And he'd seen Sir Richard Gawthorpe. His nemesis.

*That* was what was making him run. Not knowing what the hell was going on.

But why had McGee let him go? Why hadn't he stopped him?

Danny knew there was no point in trying to sort out his thoughts. Not while he was running like this, one foot banging painfully down on the concrete, followed by the other foot. He had to run. Find a safe place. Then he could think.

## *NOWHERE TO RUN*

Danny ran for five minutes. Without stopping. Without looking back. It was the only way he could cope with the fear he was feeling. He ran until he reached another set of steps going up from the river to the city.

He knew he had to keep running. Run. Don't look to see if they're catching up with you.

He took three steps up at a time.

When he reached the top he had no choice but to stop for air. His chest felt like it was being gripped in a vice. He squatted and looked back down the way he'd come.

He expected to see no one. He expected to have outrun anyone who was coming after him. And, really, he thought, they had no reason to chase him anyway. He was just a boy. There were two England goalkeepers on the steps Danny had left. Why would they come after him?

He exhaled.

Then he saw two men. Both in black. Both coming round the bend in the river at full speed. Both looking straight at him.

Danny retched. He thought he was being sick, but it

was just a nervous reaction. He stood up, knowing he didn't have enough oxygen in his blood to really run. The staircase had shattered him.

But he had no choice.

He turned. What were his options?

He had only one. Cross the road. To the other side. To a big red 'M'. A Metro station. The underground.

Danny could hear the men on the steps now. Their footsteps pounding.

He wanted to cry. He couldn't go forward. The traffic was horrific. He couldn't go backwards or sideways or stay where he was.

He racked his brain for *something*. Some novel where the character had escaped over six lanes of traffic. But that was ridiculous: he could remember no such scene. What did come into his mind was a computer game he'd played when he was a kid. A very little kid. *Frogger*. You had to move a frog across a stream, jumping him on to logs. Then get it across a road without it being flattened by articulated lorries. All you had to do was judge the gaps – and go for it.

So he did.

The first three lanes were OK. He found gaps quite easily.

It was the fourth lane that threw him. And the dozens of horns being sounded at him. This wasn't rush-hour traffic going at ten miles an hour. This was high-speed traffic. And all of it switching lanes at random.

Danny had three lanes left to cross. But he was paralysed in the middle. He looked ahead. St Basil's Cathedral. He longed to be able to walk up to it like he'd had the chance before. He looked back. There were the two men laughing. And pointing at him.

*They think I'm dead*, Danny thought. *They think I can't do this and a car's going to run me over.*

So Danny put his arms up. Like the traffic cop. He stared the drivers in the eyes and held both palms out like he was supposed to be here stopping the traffic. The car in the fourth lane slowed. Danny walked in front of it. The car in the fifth lane slowed. Danny walked in front of that too. But the next car in the sixth lane – a red car – did not stop. Or slow down. And it was coming at him fast. So Danny dived through the air, lifting off. It was all he could do.

He expected to be hit by the car. And when the pain came he knew he had, until he looked down to see he had actually made it. He had hit the pavement. The fast red car was long gone.

Danny got up.

What were the men in black doing?

They were still on the other side of the road. One was trying to dodge across the first lane, but kept running back, unable even to make it to the second lane. The other was on his mobile phone.

Danny knew what *that* meant.

Reinforcements. Another black people-carrier full of men.

He had to get away. And he knew exactly where.

## JOURNEY TO THE CENTRE OF THE EARTH

Danny had been on the tube in London – and in Newcastle – back home. If Moscow's tube was anything like London's, it'd be a mass of people rushing to and fro. Impossible to follow people because of all the bodies and confusion. He hoped.

Danny ran to the tube station he'd seen from the other side of the road. The building didn't look like a tube station. It was more like the entrance to a museum or a library.

Danny hesitated and looked over his shoulder.

Were the men coming? Had they made it over the road?

Yes.

And they were coming his way. They'd seen him too. One of them pointed.

So he ran. Through the heavy wooden doors into the underground station. Past a small crowd of Muscovites. Vaulting the turnstiles, ignoring the shouts of a woman. Something in Russian. *Stop*, he imagined. Then down the escalator. More shouts. But he was going fast now. And he wasn't going to stop.

The escalator was a shock, difficult not to stop and admire. It was seriously long and seriously steep. Not like a small escalator in a shopping centre at home, carrying you up from one floor to the next, this one was at least four hundred metres down, a journey to the centre of the earth.

But he kept on running. Hoping he wouldn't turn his ankle. Or break his leg. Or just fall.

What Danny needed was a train waiting for him.

And there was.

He was a lucky man.

He headed left and dashed on to the train just as the doors shut. Danny stood and waited. He almost expected something to happen now. Something involving the men chasing him. Or the people who'd shouted at him as he ran – without paying – through the underground station.

Then he felt the train accelerate away from the station. He'd got away. Only now did he notice what the underground station was like.

It had a huge arched ceiling. It had statues. It had oil paintings. And – most strangely of all – it had dozens of chandeliers hanging down from the ceiling.

Danny blinked. This had to be a dream. Underground stations weren't supposed to look like this. They were supposed to be filthy and dark and full of adverts.

Then the outside of the train was plunged into

darkness and Danny noticed the reflection of dozens of people all staring at him.

When the train arrived in the next station Danny had got his breath back. He decided it was best to get off the train as soon as he could. Then on to another.

He followed hundreds of people through a series of tunnels. This tube station was even more spectacular than the other. Beautiful statues. Stained-glass windows. Massive marble columns. He *had* to be dreaming. Or maybe he was dead – and this was the afterlife.

For Danny it didn't matter if he was dead or dreaming or neither: he wanted to get out of here. Find somewhere safe. If he could.

He reached another platform, waited a minute, then jumped on to another train.

He had no idea where he was or where he was going. All the words on the tube maps and guides were in Russian script. They meant nothing to him. He wouldn't have been able to decipher them even if he'd heard of the place they were describing. He just needed to be going. Moving. Running away.

## THE KREMLIN

'Everything is in place, Sir Richard?' Dmitri Tupolev asked.

'Almost,' the Englishman replied.

'Almost?'

The two men were sitting in a large and elaborately decorated room at the top of a tower overlooking a high wall from which they could gaze down into Red Square.

Sir Richard stared down at the square before he answered. The people looked so small out there. He wondered which leaders of Russia had stared out through this window. And on to what great moments in history?

'Is there something that displeases you, Sir Richard?'

'The boy.'

'Ah, the boy my men chased?' Tupolev almost laughed. 'He was just a boy. He ran so fast he must have been scared very much. He will say nothing. And if he does, no one will believe him. What did he see? An accident?'

Sir Richard frowned. He never expected to think this: but he felt Tupolev was being naïve.

Tupolev spoke again. 'The important facts are: McGee has agreed to accept our offer. And Skatie is unable to take part.' Tupolev smiled. 'All we have to do is sit back and enjoy the game.'

Sir Richard nodded.

'You're not having second thoughts, are you, my friend?' Tupolev said. 'Not becoming all patriotic, wanting England to win?'

Sir Richard smiled. 'No. That is the last of my worries.'

'Then it *is* the boy?'

'Yes, the boy.'

Tupolev just looked at Sir Richard. He was waiting for an explanation.

Sir Richard looked around the room. This had to be the finest room he had ever seen – and he had seen some serious rooms. The walls were gold. Sir Richard didn't doubt for a minute that it was real gold. The ceiling was decorated like an enormous oil painting. Beautiful. And there was a series of large ornaments on a shelf around the wall. Eggs. Small, medium and large eggs. Each was painted or bejewelled. Sir Richard knew that these were Fabergé eggs, each probably worth thousands of pounds. Some maybe more.

'There is something I have not told you about England,' he said. 'About my . . . difficulties.'

Tupolev nodded, but said nothing.

Sir Richard knew he should go on. 'When the Roberts affair came out . . .'

'Yes?'

'The main reason I . . . failed . . . was that boy.'

'*That* boy?'

'Yes, *that* boy. Although you will have read about other things, it was a boy – *that* boy – who got in my way.'

'How can a boy . . . ?'

'He's a special boy.'

'But he was lucky? He found out your plans?'

'No, I don't think so. I think he worked everything out. Then tried to stop me.'

'A boy, Sir Richard? Maybe once he was lucky. But now he is no threat. Not against me and my . . . people. And you, of course.'

'I hope not, Dmitri. But it is important you should know about him.'

Tupolev picked up a phone. 'Do you want him captured or simply dead?' he enquired.

'Sorry?'

'The boy? I will send out my best men today and tonight. It will be just a matter of time. My men know the city and all its ways.' Tupolev paused. 'Dead or alive?'

Sir Richard knew he shouldn't stall or appear weak. He needed Tupolev to see that he was a decisive and strong man.

'Dead,' he said.

Tupolev began to dial, his expression completely unchanged.

If the two men had looked down into Red Square at that moment they might have seen a small figure walking briskly from left to right, across the front of the famous GUM department store, a building that looked more like a cathedral.

Danny had emerged from the Metro and was heading for the swirling towers of St Basil's Cathedral.

Sanctuary.

When Holt had told him the story about how the cathedral had played its part in history, he had listened with some interest. But now the story meant everything to him. This cathedral was to be *his* sanctuary, his hiding-place, the place he could feel safe, away from the men in black, the guns under their jackets that he had been so terrified by earlier.

He walked quickly across the square, not looking up at the Kremlin. Nor at the mausoleum that seemed so trivial to him now. Now that he felt his life was in danger.

He needed time to think. Time to work out what he had seen and what it meant. McGee. Skatie. The men in black. Sir Richard. Had it really been him? Then he needed to call to ask for Holt's help.

As Danny approached the cathedral he looked back.

What he saw terrified him.

Through a large fortified gate at the near end of the square, a group of eight men, all dressed in black, had emerged. One of them finished a phone conversation and snapped his phone shut. Danny could see him issuing orders to the other men.

The men split into pairs. Heading off in different directions.

Danny knew who they were. He recognized the one giving orders. And he was pretty sure who they were looking for.

Him.

He moved quickly into the cathedral, buying a ticket at the entrance. Could he find somewhere to hide? Or someone to help him? Or would he be thrown out, back on to the street where the men in black would find him in no time?

It was – without doubt – the strangest cathedral he'd been in. Not huge echoing space, but a honeycomb of rooms and narrow passages. Everything was decorated: the walls, the ceilings, the floors. Danny was awestruck. He'd never seen anything like this before.

Inside, Danny decided to walk round the cathedral as if admiring it. But this was a reconnaissance. He had to clear his head and think. He stopped every minute or so to gaze at a panel or a ceiling. But as he looked, he saw nothing. His fear of capture was so overwhelming that he felt like his senses weren't working. His heart was going so fast he felt sick.

So, where to hide?

Behind a massive painting that was leaning against the wall of the cathedral? No, he'd be seen there.

In one of the rooms that were part of the strange labyrinth? No, there was no place to hide.

Through a door, maybe leading downstairs to the cellars? But all the doorways were locked or blocked by glass panels. And anyway, it was too risky. He could end up locked down there all night.

Then he saw it. Back at the entrance. Somewhere he *could* lie down. A tomb. It looked like a four-poster bed. It was decorated with images and gold, metal pots hanging down. It was the tomb of St Basil. And, behind it, there was a gap, just big enough for him to slip behind.

*Perfect*, Danny thought.

It was a place to hide in case the men in black came searching for him. And very possibly a place to spend the night.

Danny climbed round the tomb and crouched. Then, after a minute, lay down and breathed out, closing his eyes.

He had a million questions.

Why would Matt McGee attack Robert Skatie?

Was he sure he'd seen Sir Richard Gawthorpe?

And, if so, what was he doing on the steps by the river?

And would the team of men come looking for him in here?

Every question begged another question.

When Danny opened his eyes he was stunned to see the inside of a tower above him. At the top of the tower, staring down at him, a massive painting of Jesus.

At first it surprised him. But then it made him feel better. Somehow. Like it meant he was going to be safe.

Once Danny was settled – and was sure that there were no people nearby – he took out his phone and called Holt. Holt would get him out of this situation.

Danny dialled his number. He put his ear to the phone, hoping to hear Holt's familiar voice. Even leaving a message would be OK.

But the line beeped in a way Danny hadn't heard it beep before and then a woman's voice started babbling Russian at him. Danny listened, hoping for some miracle. But there was nothing.

Danny tried Holt again.

Silence.

Then he tried it with the UK dialling code. Maybe he needed to do that.

Nothing again.

Now Danny had only one option. To stay in the cathedral. There was no way he would dare go out on the street again.

It was getting dark. It looked like this was where he was going to spend the night.

# WEDNESDAY

## THE LONGEST NIGHT

It was dark and – if Danny was honest with himself – scary in the cathedral. He had hunkered down. No security guard had see him behind the tomb. He was definitely safe. So long as there weren't any ghosts.

Danny frowned. He had enough to cope with – security guards, private armies, homicidal ex-football chairmen and spies – without imagining ghosts.

The cathedral was eerie. But Danny tried not to think about it. About the fact that he was alone in a centuries-old building. About the fact that he was lying metres away from the dead body in the tomb. About the men he believed would be out there, looking for him, maybe even waiting for him.

Knowing that he was here for the night, Danny got as comfortable as he could, using his rolled-up jacket for a pillow. It was still dark. Very dark. He was exhausted – and soon fell asleep.

Danny woke some hours later, his phone buzzing.

He had two texts. One from Charlotte. One from his sister.

He surprised himself by opening the one from his sister first.

**Hey runt – how's it going? Hope England win 2morrow. Not. Em xxx**

Danny rested his head on his jacket and smiled. What was that all about? This was as close his sister could get to being nice. He paused before looking at Charlotte's text. He wasn't sure what he was feeling about his sister. But it was something like *missing* her.

Danny grimaced and opened Charlotte's text:

**D. Text me now. RU ok? Need to hear from U. C xxxxxx**

Danny texted back immediately:

**Am fine. Sleeping in a cathedral. V nice. Don't worry. I'll txt a.m. from stadium. D xxxxxx**

Then Danny heard what he thought were footsteps. He opened his eyes and lifted his head very slightly above the rim of the tomb. Had he given himself away somehow by texting?

Nobody there.

It was 3 a.m. Who would be looking round the

cathedral now? There was barely any light coming in through the entrance.

No one. Not even Jesus's face gazing down at him.

He must be hearing things.

The guards had locked the doors at 5 p.m. All of them slamming like they were never going to be opened again. Leaving Danny in the cathedral alone, he was sure.

More footsteps. Danny looked again.

No one.

Danny was terrified. He was alone in a strange church in a strange city. He was possibly being hunted down by the private army of a billionaire with a reputation for murder and his only friend in the city was too busy to help him and oblivious to where he was. And now he was hearing things. *And* he was hungry. And thirsty.

He looked over the top of the tomb.

Nothing.

Nobody.

They can't have been footsteps, he decided.

He settled back to rest – aware he'd probably not get any more sleep.

'Daaaaa-nnyyyyy?'

Danny woke.

Where was he?

Then he remembered. Of course, how could he forget: behind a tomb in a cathedral in the middle of the night! He was confused. And scared.

Had he really heard someone call his name?

He waited. Nothing more. He must have dreamed it.

'Daaaaa-nnyyyyyy.'

Danny stopped breathing. Utter terror. Was it whoever had been making the footsteps? Or was it the men in black? They were the only ones who might know his name. Or was it . . . Sir Richard? Come for revenge. And whoever it was, why were they doing it at four – was it? – in the morning?

Danny looked at his watch. It was eleven. Eleven a.m.! Where had the time gone? It *wasn't* the middle of the night. Light was flooding the cathedral, with Jesus fully illuminated gazing down at him.

He kept his head low, but peeped over the side of the tomb.

He saw the figure of a man standing alone in the entrance, light streaming in through the door behind him.

The man put his hands to his mouth and called again. 'Daaaaa-nny!'

It was Holt. Definitely Holt.

Danny paused for a second. How had Holt found him? Had someone seen him and told Holt? No. Who would do that? For a second the idea that Holt wasn't all he seemed flashed into Danny's mind. The idea that he was a double agent, that he was involved with the attacks on the players – and with Sir Richard. Could it be possible? Was that how he'd found him?

Danny shook his head. No way. That just wasn't possible. His gut feeling was that he was an idiot to think such things. He was just being paranoid. He jumped up from behind the tomb just as Holt was making to leave.

'Anton?' Danny called.

Holt turned to him. Danny saw his face open out into a smile, a genuine pleased-to-see-you smile.

There was no way he was corrupt. How could he have thought that?

'Come on,' Holt said, grabbing Danny's arm, leading him roughly out of the cathedral.

'What?'

'Out of here. I've got a car. A hire car. It's round the back of the cathedral.'

Holt had broken into a quick walk.

Danny ran alongside him.

'Don't run,' Holt hissed. 'Don't draw attention.' Holt glanced up at the Kremlin. 'Something's going on.'

'How do you know something's going on?' Danny said, breathless – and still stiff, after a night on a stone floor.

'You disappeared. You're nosy. I know you're up to

something. And you look like a hunted animal. Am I right?'

And Danny felt like there were a thousand eyes on him. 'Yes.'

Holt nodded. They walked quickly, side by side until they reached a small white car.

'Get in.'

Danny took the door handle and slipped into the car.

As Holt reversed the car, Danny looked up at St Basil's. In the morning light it looked magnificent.

Its colours.

Its spiralling towers.

He couldn't believe that he had hated it before. It was beautiful and now he could only think of it as one of his favourite places in the world.

## *TO THE LUZHNIKI*

'How did you know where I'd be?' Danny asked, once Holt had eased the car into the mass of traffic streaming over a bridge, the gears crunching worryingly.

Holt shrugged. 'It was a hunch. We talked about it being a place of sanctuary.'

'Thanks.'

Holt paused. Then he said, 'I've been up all night. Worrying sick. I sat in that bloody lobby for hours. I thought you were . . . I don't know.' He had his eyes on the road all the time he said this.

Danny felt ashamed. Although there was nothing he could have done. He thought about using his phone as an excuse, but there was no point.

The roads were tail-to-tail cars, vans, trucks, bikes, buses and more cars. It was impossible for Holt to move from one lane to another. Larger vehicles bullied their smaller car if he tried to move either left or right. Holt cursed as he missed his turning. Cars beeped.

He thrust a map into Danny's hands. 'I'm lost. Absolutely stuffed. Can you map read? Please. It's enough trying to deal with this traffic.'

Danny nodded. He *could* map read. He spent most

car journeys reading maps, whether his mum wanted him to or not.

Danny quickly worked out where they were. 'Keep going along here,' he instructed. 'It splits. We need to move to the right, so we're in a good lane.' Danny knew where they were going: the Luzhniki Stadium. Where Russia played their home World Cup ties.

Holt nodded. 'OK?' he said.

'I'm sorry.' Danny looked behind them at a car beeping its horn. 'About going missing.'

'Nutters,' Holt muttered.

'What?' Danny said, casting his eyes to the road behind them. And looking back, he saw what was on the back seat. Two files. One read TUPOLEV, DMITRI. The other GAWTHORPE, SIR RICHARD.

'Why have you got those files on the back seat?'

There was a long pause.

'I think it's time to come clean,' Holt said.

'Why would you have a file on Sir Richard Gawthorpe?' Danny asked.

'Sir Richard,' Holt said. 'He's in Russia.'

So it *had* been Sir Richard on the steps. Danny was not going mad. But what was the link, the missing piece in the jigsaw? It was whatever Anton was looking into – and had been hiding from Danny. That had to be it.

'So why the files? Why are you looking into these two?'

Holt sighed again. 'I should have told you,' he said.

'What?'

'I've been doing a piece on Tupolev and Sir Richard trying to buy City.'

'You *knew* Sir Richard was around?'

'I didn't *know*,' Holt corrected him. 'I knew someone English was involved with Tupolev. But I did have my suspicions.'

Danny nodded.

'So I was looking into it,' Holt went on. 'And I saw him. In a hotel. Two days ago. When I said I had to go and interview someone. I'm starting to put together a picture.'

'They're trying to buy City?' Danny asked.

'They *will* buy City,' Holt replied. Then he braked suddenly and looked at Danny. 'But there's something else.'

'What?'

'Robert Skatie had an accident last night. He's out of the game. And I'm sure it's linked to all this.'

Danny nodded again. Vigorously. 'It is linked.'

'What? What do you mean?'

'The whole thing. Tupolev. Sir Richard. McGee. Skatie. Even Finn.'

Holt said nothing.

'McGee attacked Skatie,' Danny said solemnly.

Holt shook his head. 'No way.'

'He did.'

'You've no evidence.'

'I saw it,' Danny said. 'I filmed it.'

'Yeah, right.'

'I *did*,' Danny insisted. 'That's why I ended up in that cathedral. I was running from some of Tupolev's men. They were there. And so was Sir Richard.'

Holt carried on driving. His eyes were flashing all over the road. 'Look. Did you know? Skatie was named as keeper yesterday morning. For the match. That'd be why McGee did it – maybe?'

And suddenly it all clicked into place for Danny. Tupolev and Sir Richard. McGee and Skatie. And Finn.

'Sir Richard wants City.'

'Yeah.' Now it was Holt's turn to nod.

'And he needs an investor.'

'Yeah.'

'Tupolev wants to invest in a Premiership team.'

'Yeah.'

'So Sir Richard gets him on his side – by promising to nobble the England keeper, so that Russia win the games against England.'

Holt slapped his hand to his forehead. 'That's it,' he said.

'So they get to Finn,' Danny continued. 'He refuses to give in – and as a result he's involved in a car accident, where he could quite easily have been killed.'

'Right.'

'Then they get to McGee at the party.'

'Yeah.'

'But Skatie is picked to play in the game.'

'Yeah!'

'So McGee attacks Skatie.'

'But that's what I don't get,' Holt frowned. 'Why does McGee attack Skatie so he can betray his country?'

'That's what *I* don't get,' Danny agreed, feeling uneasy. 'It could be that he wanted whatever Tupolev and Sir Richard have offered him.'

'Money,' Holt said. 'For his debts.'

'I don't know . . .'

'It's obvious.'

'But when I saw McGee attack Skatie, McGee told me to run for it. He saved me. Sort of.'

Holt drove through some lights, glancing left, then right. 'That doesn't mean he's not taking the cash,' he said.

'But it means he's not all bad,' Danny maintained. 'There was something about him. I'm not sure he's corrupt. We have to give him the benefit of the doubt.'

'You reckon?' Holt said. 'That's the last piece in the jigsaw for me. McGee attacking Skatie. I can finish my article now – get it in the papers tomorrow. They'll give me the front page for this.'

'Right.'

'Hey?'

'Right. *Turn* right.'

Holt took a sudden turn at some lights, careering across the path of several cars.

'We have to give him a chance,' Danny said, thoughtful for a second. 'He gave me one.'

'Maybe.'

'Left.'

'Left,' Holt repeated. 'Left here?'

'Yes.'

Holt took a left. And suddenly they saw the stadium.

There were already hundreds of fans standing around outside a Metro station. Several tables set up selling England and Russia flags and shirts.

Holt drove slowly through the crowds.

'Right here.'

'What?'

'Turn. Right. Here.'

Holt grimaced and manoeuvred the hire car into the right-hand lane.

'The main thing for me is to get you safely home, Danny. If you *have* got a private army after you, then that's my priority. It's my fault you're here.'

'So what are we going to do?' Danny was nervous again after the mention of private armies. 'And why are we driving to the Luzhniki Stadium so soon?'

'Hear me out,' Holt said. 'The stadium is the safest place we can be. There's massive security. And – if the security is corrupt – there's the world's media around us. We get there hours before anyone would expect to see us there. Find a safe place. Watch the game. Then join the official England coach out of there.'

'Do you reckon?'

'I can't see a safer way of getting you out of here. If they *are* after you – which I'm not convinced about, but I'll trust you on that – then there's no way we should show up at the airport. Or outside the British embassy.'

Danny nodded, but said nothing.

The stadium looked magnificent. Like a cross between the old Wembley and the new. Its outside was old stone, looking solid. But inside Danny could see a glass roof in a perfect oval shape.

There weren't many cars around, but there were several media vans. Some with satellite dishes on top. People sat on their steps drinking cups of tea or coffee.

Holt parked up in a mostly empty car park down the side of a sports centre.

'Let's walk.'

'OK.'

Holt cleared his throat. 'When we're in there,' he said, 'make sure you stay in the press area. You'll be safe there. Don't stray out of it and we'll be all right. OK?'

Danny nodded.

As they approached the stadium, Danny saw a huge statue of a man.

'Wonder who that is?' Holt said.

'Lenin,' Danny replied.

'How do you know that?'

'We nearly became friends,' Danny said, smiling.

Holt said nothing, nodding. Then he pointed to their left. 'There,' he said. 'The press entrance. Once we're in there we'll be safe.'

Danny nodded too. Though he wasn't convinced.

## THE STADIUM

Danny had never seen a football stadium press area before. He'd seen a press conference at City, but nothing like this. This was international standard.

There were dozens of desks, all hooked up to the Internet. Comfy seats. And a spacious bar. *Everything* was there for the press. They were treated like Danny expected players to be treated. There was already a woman asking if Holt wanted a drink. And Danny.

Danny asked for a Coke. Holt, water.

On the upper floor of the press area you could watch the match through an enormous pane of glass. Or you could sit in the stands in a series of orange seats with a desk area in front of each, which were also hooked up to the Internet and phone lines.

Danny headed upstairs to have a look over the pitch.

He looked across the perfect rectangle of synthetic grass and three layers of seats: yellow, orange and red, the upper tier. All the seats were still empty. Above them, a huge curved roof cast a shadow over the pitch. Around the pitch were huge banks of snow and what looked like wheelbarrows to carry it away.

Danny moved down the aisle to have a closer look

at the pitch, not seeing the two men waiting above him.

Both men were wearing black. They'd been trailing Anton Holt all day. Their boss had insisted on it. As soon as they saw Holt emerge from St Basil's – with Danny – they'd been ready, just two cars behind them as they drove from Red Square to the stadium.

They'd followed him all the way.

'*Mi atakovat' yego tyepyerye?*' said the first man. *Shall we attack him now?*

'*Nyet, zhurnalist, tam*,' the other replied, as Holt emerged behind Danny. *No, the journalist is there.*

'Danny. Come on. Keep a low profile,' Holt said.

'I was just looking at the pitch.'

Holt pulled Danny in by the arm as the two men observed them.

'Save it until the players come for their warm-up,' Holt said. 'You never know who's about. Play it safe.'

An hour later the England squad emerged. A string of players jogging out on to the pitch, gazing up at the stands and the pale blue sky above.

Holt had been tapping away on his laptop non-stop since they'd come back in. Working up his piece about Tupolev and his theories about what was going on with the City take-over. Feeding in Danny's material.

'Come on,' Danny urged.

Holt sighed. 'Just a minute.'

'No way,' Danny said. 'We need to talk to him.'

They waited in the tunnel, a tube of glossy plastic that led out to the edge of the pitch. Players came and went. Peter Day. Stuart Lane. And Phil White. But not Matt McGee.

Danny and Holt waited. Three or four of the players said hello to Holt. A couple nodded and smiled at Danny. The atmosphere was calm and friendly.

Eventually Matt McGee appeared and walked past them.

'Matt,' Danny called out.

McGee smiled and waved at first. Then he stopped and doubled back.

'All right?' he said. Very guarded.

'Hello, Matt,' Holt said.

'Listen, lads –' McGee began.

Danny broke in. He wanted to be straightforward. 'We know about Tupolev,' he said. 'And what he wants you to do.'

'You *think* you know,' McGee said, with a sharper, but quieter, tone of voice.

'We know about the attack on Skatie too,' Holt said. 'Danny here wants to give you the chance to explain, even though he saw –'

McGee shook his head. He breathed in, then said, 'Leave it.'

'How can we?' Holt demanded.

'Please,' McGee said. 'Leave it. You don't know what you're dealing with.'

'Dmitri Tupolev. Sir Richard Gawthorpe,' Danny said, to push him.

'Sir Rich–' McGee stopped himself.

'Yes. Remember him?'

'What's he doing here –' McGee stopped himself again.

Holt said nothing.

Danny decided he had to speak up. 'I don't think it's true,' he said. 'About you.'

Holt looked at him. Danny thought he was going to contradict, but he didn't.

'Keep thinking that,' McGee said.

'Why should we, Matt?' Holt said. 'The evidence –'

'Anton. Do you value your life?' McGee said.

'What the hell does that mean?' Holt stepped back a pace.

'I'm not threatening you,' McGee said, putting his hands up. 'I'm saying if you value your life, then keep out of it. Don't write a word. Not yet.'

'*That's* a threat.'

'Not from me,' McGee said and turned to walk down the tunnel. 'Not from me,' he said again. Then he was gone.

## *PRE-MATCH TENSION*

Danny had spent most of the afternoon watching people. Unable to go anywhere and with Holt tapping away on his laptop, he had no option. He'd had two Cokes and a sandwich: now he was feeling jumpy.

Danny had tried to persuade Holt that he shouldn't condemn McGee until the match, until he *did* throw the game. But Holt was convinced that McGee was going to let Russia win. Danny tried arguing with him for a while, but got nowhere.

So Danny sat and thought: trying to sift through everything he knew, thinking what he could do next.

A couple of hours before kick-off he got a text from Paul.

**What d'y reckon? 2-2? P**

Danny replied.

**Depends on McG. If he plays bad, we lose. D**

Throughout the afternoon more football writers arrived. Many of them Russian, who nodded a greeting, then got on with connecting their laptops up to their desks. And talking to each other in low voices, occasionally laughing at each other's remarks.

But something had changed in the atmosphere too. Danny started to feel that tingling he got in his shoulders – the butterflies he got in his chest – when he was on the way to watch City back home. Pre-match tension. The best feeling in the world. And he was surprised that it made him think of his dad. And he had a disturbing thought: this would be the first match he'd been to *without* his dad. Ever.

His tingling turned to sadness. Or loneliness. He wasn't sure. One thing he knew was that he missed his dad.

It just didn't feel right. Being here without him.

When Holt had to leave to make some phone calls, out of earshot of the other journalists, Danny used Holt's laptop to check his emails. He drafted an email to his dad. *Hello. Wish you were here.* That sort of thing. Then he surfed the Net and found a match preview.

England go into today's vital qualifier only needing a draw to keep their World Cup campaign on track. After beating Russia at Wembley, one point each would leave England two points clear of a Russia team running out of time to catch England. But England have promised to play an expansive game, and not to defend, which, in the manager's own words, would be 'an invitation to the Russians to score'. The World Cup finals beckon and . . .

Danny felt a surge of excitement. Even though he had worries – how he was going to get out of this country being the first of many – he loved the football, loved the prospect of watching a team he supported playing for something so important.

However, there was something else on Danny's mind too: he was bursting for the toilet. But Holt was still away.

Danny decided to risk it, even though Holt wouldn't want him to. He needed to go. So long as he didn't leave the press area, he'd be OK. That was the deal with Holt, wasn't it?

As it happened, though, the gents appeared to be locked, so Danny had to go right down to the ground floor, under the stadium, to find a toilet. Out of the press area, but still in a part of the stadium closed to the public. Past some offices and a small gym with exercise bikes and treadmills.

As he was about to enter the toilets, a man came out.

The man nodded, held the door open for Danny, then disappeared down a corridor. As he did, two men emerged from the pitch area. The two men in black. One of them pointed to the toilets. The other nodded. They'd seen Danny go in.

The two men had been given orders. Deal with the boy. Direct orders from Tupolev – which meant you got the job done.

But the men were unaware that Matt McGee was watching them and had seen Danny go into the gents too.

The men in black went towards the toilet door, looking up and down the corridor. Checking. Now they could finish the piece of work they'd meant to deal with on the banks of the Moskva. They pushed the door open gently. No need to warn their target they'd arrived.

But that was when they saw Matt McGee running towards them; he rushed past and along the corridor, possibly out of the stadium.

The two men looked at each other, puzzled for a second, then they sprinted after McGee. He was their priority. If they let him slip away their boss would kill them. Quite literally.

They'd get the boy later.

In the gents, Danny heard the door and expected to see someone come in after him, but no one did. He heard the sound of running too, but assumed it was the players coming back from warming up.

The two men in black watched McGee double back down the corridor, head down the tunnel and run a lap of the pitch, in front of some England fans, there in good time, as Danny came out of the toilets and went back upstairs.

'Where've you been?'

'Toilet.'

Holt sighed. 'You should have waited for me.'

'You'd gone. I was desperate.'

'Where did you go?'

'Under the stand. It was fine.'

Holt nodded. 'OK,' he said. 'Anyway, I've got us a lift on the England coach later. Back to the airport and fast track on to the plane. I talked to a mate at the FA.'

'Great.'

'So all we have to do is stay in the press room – before and during the match. OK?'

'Yep.'

Holt smiled. He looked more relaxed.

'How's the article going?' Danny asked.

'Good,' Holt said. 'Do you want to read it?'

'Sure,' Danny said.

'It'd be a help. There's lots of your stuff in it. And it

might jog your memory.' Holt rubbed his hands together. 'If we get out of here this is going on the front page on Friday.'

Danny sat down to read.

## ENGLAND WORLD CUP MATCH FIXED – EXCLUSIVE

### ANTON HOLT IN MOSCOW

Now the smoke of battle has cleared after England's World Cup defeat last night, the *Evening Post* can report something that will shake the world game to its core: Russia versus England was fixed.

The *Evening Post*'s football reporter, Anton Holt, has been working on a piece of investigative journalism for several weeks.

The plain truth is: Russia bought the game.

This is the story of how they did that.

The plot to ensure that Russia are ahead of England in Group F of World Cup qualifying has involved a trail of deceit that takes a lot to believe. But – using eye-witness accounts and some remarkable mobile-phone video footage – the evidence speaks for itself.

Bring together a Russian oligarch, a disgraced English football chairman, three international goal-keepers and the illegal take-over of a top English

Premiership club and you have the recipe for the football scandal to top all football scandals.

### The Russian Oligarch

Dmitri Tupolev is a well-known figure in Russian football circles. He is a major political figure with a seat in the Russian parliament, the Duma. He is the world's fourteenth richest man, worth around £300 billion. He owns the top Russian and Ukrainian football clubs.

But Dmitri Tupolev wanted more.

He wanted a Premiership club, a team from the best football league in the world. England.

And when he met a former English football chairman and owner – one who was keen to get back into football – his entrée into the Premiership seemed a matter of time.

Except for one thing. His part of the deal.

Dmitri Tupolev was willing to hand over £400 million to buy the English club in question. But first he wanted something in return.

A favour.

What sort of favour?

Dmitri Tupolev wanted his English partner to make sure Russia finished above England in Group F of the World Cup qualifiers.

He would need an Englishman so unprincipled and dastardly he was willing to commit what is as close as you can get to treason in footballing terms.

Who?

Sir Richard Gawthorpe.

Remember him?

## The English Chairman

Sir Richard Gawthorpe disappeared in June this year when his plot to make money from kidnapping his own player at City backfired.

After his plan to make money from England striker Sam Roberts went sour, Gawthorpe vanished, leaving behind his £300 million fortune and his famous red Mercedes.

No one knew where he was, or if he would ever resurface. Or even if he was still among the living. But this reporter can confirm he saw him in Moscow. In the Cosmonaut Hotel on 17 October.

In addition, another member of the paper's staff took footage of Gawthorpe on the banks of Moscow's famous river, the Moskva.

He was here. No question. We have the proof.

### THE SWEETENER

It is clear that Sir Richard and Dmitri Tupolev are working together to buy City and make them into the most powerful club team in Europe.

But first, the sweetener.

This newspaper is suggesting that before he would hand over the money, Dmitri Tupolev asked Sir Richard Gawthorpe to get to England and City goalkeeper Matt McGee. To make him throw the World Cup qualifier between Russia and England.

McGee was approached at a reception for the England party on the outskirts of Moscow earlier this week.

Secret film recorded this exchange:

Tupolev: A penalty in the first half. A misjudged cross in the second. Yes?

McGee: [*No reply.*]

Tupolev: Yes?

McGee: I heard what you said.

[Note: GAP FOR DESCRIPTION OF McGEE'S 'ERRORS' IN GAME]

Further footage shows a scene on the banks of the Moskva: Matt McGee attacking Robert Skatie.

McGee can be seen pushing Skatie down a flight of steps.

And who is seen at the top of the steps, looking on?

Sir Richard Gawthorpe.

### MATT MCGEE

Matt McGee is a likeable man. But he is flawed.

He is a gambler: with reported debts of over one million.

He mixes with known criminals.

He has a conviction for handling counterfeit money.

McGee's flaws are what made him vulnerable. He was an easy target for Tupolev and Gawthorpe. The final piece in the deal that Sir Richard Gawthorpe struck with Dmitri Tupolev to cheat football fans across England.

### TOMORROW

Gawthorpegate: the details, the pictures and access to the films online.

Danny looked up at Holt, who was staring at him.

'Well?' Holt asked.

'Please don't,' Danny said.

'What?'

'There's too much guesswork.'

'Danny,' Holt stood up. 'It's based on your films. What you saw.'

'But I still don't think McGee could do it.'

'Why on earth not? It's clear.'

'Because I have a gut feeling. And because the match hasn't happened yet.'

'I'll fill those bits in after the game. But I'll get this off to the paper now – or they won't hold the front page for it.'

'Wait.'

'Why? Don't you want this on the news pages? Aren't you disgusted?'

'Not yet, please.' Danny was feeling more and more uncomfortable with Holt. The article had gone to his head. He wanted to be the famous journalist who broke the most dramatic story in 150 years of association football.

Holt was still shaking his head when Danny said, 'And if McGee plays well and England win, what then?'

'He won't. You have *seen* the films you made?'

'Yes, but McGee didn't actually say yes, did he? He might not do it. How would your boss react if he held the front page and printed ten times as many papers as usual, then England won?'

Holt frowned. He looked like a little kid who'd had his exciting plans frustrated.

'Wait,' Danny begged. 'Please.'

Holt slammed his laptop shut. He looked out of the window. He reminded Danny of his sister: when she hadn't got her own way.

Neither said anything for three minutes. Danny thought it best to leave it, wait for Holt to say something.

'You're right,' Holt said eventually.

Danny nodded. But deep down he wondered if he *was* right. They'd soon see: kick-off was approaching.

## *FIRST HALF*

The tension in the stadium was overwhelming as the players came on to the pitch.

Danny had been able to watch the fans arriving through windows in the back of the press area. English and Russians mingling and talking. The stadium was in a lightly wooded park, on the edge of the Moskva river. A good setting.

As more and more fans arrived you could see less and less green grass. Just red, white and blue – the colours of the teams. But most of the fans were Russian. And because he was so high up, Danny could see several groups of police – or soldiers – in buses, waiting for orders if there was any trouble.

Once the game had kicked off, Danny watched through the great glass window of the press area. He'd asked Holt if he could go and sit in the press seats, but Holt had said no. It wasn't safe.

Danny accepted what Holt said. They'd got this far: there was no point in taking a risk. And it was fascinating watching the press from behind, talking into phones, typing their reports, making notes. But mostly – among the English reporters – sitting on the edge of their seats every time the ball went near either goal.

Russia were on top from the start. In the first fifteen minutes England barely got a kick. The Russian fans were singing and chanting – the atmosphere very intimidating. It was like the England players expected to lose. Very strange. Only Peter Day and Stuart Lane were having any impact at all.

A text from Paul arrived:

**This is grim. P**

Danny felt uneasy during the half. Part of it was the way England looked so second-best to Russia. But there was something else making him feel so funny.

What was it?

And then he realized: he should be commentating. To his dad. He was having a string of thoughts about the game and he wanted to speak them: like he always did at the football.

He pulled out his phone. He knew he was only meant to phone home if he had a problem. It would be expensive. But this was important.

'Dad?'

'Danny. Are you OK? Why are you phoning? What's wrong?'

Danny smiled. 'Nothing. Everything's fine. Are you following the match?'

'Yeah,' Dad said, calming down. 'On TV. Sounds like it's not going too well.'

'Is John Motson doing his stuff?'

'Yeah.' Danny heard his dad pause. 'But he's not a patch on you.'

'It's doing my head in.'

'What?'

'Not telling you what's going on.'

Dad said nothing for a minute. Then: 'Where are you?'

'In the press bit.'

'Where's that?'

'Next to the VIP area.'

'Is it good?'

'Yeah,' Danny said. 'But I'm behind glass. It's not as exciting as being in the West Stand at City.'

Danny heard his dad laugh.

'Oh no,' Danny said.

'What?'

'Russia have got a corner. Aren't you following the game?'

'Hang on . . . right. It's a corner now. We must have a delay.'

Neither Danny nor his dad spoke as the players got into position for the corner.

Danny watched in silence as the ball was lofted from

the corner flag into the England box. He saw McGee come out too soon for it and flap at the ball, then he saw the ball catch his hand and drop into the six-yard area, losing all its pace.

A Russian was on to it in a second. Hammering it home.

One–nil.

Danny said nothing. He waited until his dad cried out.

'No!' His dad paused. 'Is it a goal?'

'Yep.'

'Damn it. Sorry, Danny.'

'I'd better go,' Danny said. 'This is costing loads.'

'Call me later,' Dad said. 'I'll give you the money. It'd be good to talk. After the game. Please?'

'OK, Dad.'

Danny slipped his phone into his pocket. He watched the Russia fans leaping around, their flags swirling, their horns blaring. He looked at the VIP area too. The President of Russia was meant to be up there. Danny tried to see if he could spot him. And looked straight into the eyes of Dmitri Tupolev.

An action replay of the goal came up on a screen in front of the press area. Danny watched McGee go up, his arms raised to collect the ball, then – maybe – a slight nudge from one of the strikers, the ball falling to the other striker's feet.

Danny felt that sinking feeling he got whenever his team let in a goal. Nausea. Exhaustion. Something like that.

'What do you think?'

It was Holt, standing right behind him. Danny wondered how long he'd been there.

'He got a nudge,' Danny pointed out.

'He dropped it,' Holt said.

Danny knew what Anton was saying: McGee had let it drop on purpose.

'He wouldn't . . .'

'Wouldn't he?'

'I just can't . . . I don't –' Danny couldn't find the right words – 'believe it. But I don't know any more.'

'Let's see how it goes,' Holt said.

The first half became more and more frustrating.

The tempo was slower now. Russia – one up – were happier to play the ball around, not take any risks. They waited for England to attack, sat deep; then tried to attack on the break. But they never sent too many players up front.

Danny watched the England midfield trying to get a grip on the game. But although England had plenty of possession, there was nothing doing. The Russian defence was too deep now.

And when the ball came at the English defence the

players looked edgy. Hacking the ball away instead of passing it. Fouling players and giving away needless free kicks.

Then things looked to be getting worse. Much worse.

With seconds to go in the first half, the Russians beat the English offside trap, leaving a Russian winger one-on-one with McGee in goal. McGee dashed out of his area to fling himself at the feet of the Russian.

For a moment Danny could imagine what he was going to do: bring the player down, concede a penalty, get himself sent off, end the game as a competition. If McGee did, then that was it: he *was* being bribed, corrupt.

McGee lunged to his right as the player tried to steer the ball round him. He put out his right arm and flailed at the ball. But he caught the player, not the ball.

*Just inside the penalty area*, Danny thought.

He looked down at the floor. Was that it? Had McGee done it on purpose? Two mistakes: two goals conceded, probably.

Danny watched the referee blow his whistle and go straight for his pocket. For his red card, Danny assumed. He saw McGee jump to his feet and start shouting, complaining. Then England's captain, Peter Day, pulled McGee back. Trying to stop him doing anything worse.

The referee pulled out a card: yellow.

Danny exhaled. What a relief! The game would have been dead and buried.

But now it was the Russia players complaining. Not only was McGee still on the pitch, but they hadn't been awarded a penalty. That was their argument. The referee was pointing to a spot just outside the area: he'd judged that contact had *not* been inside the penalty area.

The tall Russian striker set the ball down, turning it twice on the ground before he was happy. Then he took five deliberate steps backwards. Danny watched him breathe in and out – thinking this was another chance for McGee. If he wanted to let this in, all he had to do was dive the wrong way, make it look like he'd been fooled by the free kick.

The striker stepped up and struck it. Straight into McGee's arms. McGee hadn't moved. Had made no effort either to save it – or let it in.

Danny sat down, feeling his heart going like the clappers. He glanced up at Holt.

They shared a look, but said nothing. But Danny understood it to mean something like: is McGee trying to lose us this game, or win it?

Another text came in:

**McGee. Good save. Like I said, a draw. P**

Danny smiled. He hoped that his friend was right.

## *SECOND HALF*

*England go into the second half one down and outplayed. At the front they look ineffectual; at the back decidedly shaky. If things don't change then England will find themselves out of the qualification places for the World Cup and the English game will officially be in meltdown . . .*

Danny smiled. He was listening in on one of England's most famous radio commentators. Full of shock and horror. Like it was the end of the world. He knew that if England equalized, the same commentator would be asking for knighthoods for the whole squad.

The second half started like the first. Russia trying to finish off England. They'd had 70 per cent of the possession and were putting in a shot on goal every two minutes. Most were easy for McGee to handle. He could have spilled them or made something happen that would have looked like an honest mistake. But so far he was playing like he meant it.

And Danny was praying. As much that McGee should be honest, as that England should win.

But, as England were forced to take the game to

Russia, they became more and more stretched. And, after an hour of play, England were caught out.

This was it.

Several Russian attackers broke after a poor pass across England's midfield. It was four against two. But with a couple of high-speed passes, three against one. And – seconds later – McGee was facing two Russian strikers. With no defensive cover.

Danny stared at the scene. The game seemed to be going in slow motion. Too much time to think. To worry.

The striker with the ball drew McGee off his line, then side-footed it to the second striker, who then hit it hard and low, towards the bottom corner of the net.

Except it didn't reach the goal.

Somehow McGee pushed the ball to his side. It hit the post and spun slowly towards the line, McGee stranded on the floor. Then the first striker came in to pass the ball into the empty net.

But, when he looked up, the net wasn't empty any more. McGee had somehow lunged to his feet and blocked the Russian's shot. To loud cheers from the England fans, McGee stood and hurled the ball out to the halfway line.

Danny stood and shouted. He caught Holt's eye. They both beamed at each other. McGee was straight: there was no question. He was not going to throw the game. Holt put his thumbs up. Danny nodded back at him. He was feeling good now.

But he was shocked to hear an even louder cheer suddenly coming from the stands. The stands on the far left.

He looked at the pitch.

The England players were wheeling away from the Russian goal. The Russian keeper was on his back on his goal line. The ball behind him, caught in the net.

England had equalized.

Somehow.

Danny had *missed* it, too busy grinning at Holt.

Almost immediately Danny's mobile rang. Dad.

'How did it go in?' Dad said. 'The commentary was drowned out by the crowd.'

Danny wondered what he should say.

'I missed it.'

Honesty. Always honesty.

'You missed it,' Dad repeated. 'You go one and a half thousand miles to see a game – and you *miss* the goal. Danny!'

Danny listened to his dad laughing.

After that the game was very different. England were on top. Russia deflated.

Danny couldn't stop jumping up and down. He felt

like he was on the pitch. This had to be the best match he'd been to.

He looked up to see if he could catch Tupolev's eye. But Tupolev was not looking back at Danny. He was glaring at the pitch, his eyes as black as coal. His forehead furrowed.

Danny couldn't help but speculate about what Tupolev was thinking. Was he thinking of McGee? Of killing him? Or was he thinking about Sir Richard? What would this do to their relationship? If Holt was right about their plans to buy City.

As the match went on Danny couldn't help but keep glancing at him. He was such a magnetic figure. At one point Danny saw him pull out his phone and shout down it, snapping it shut afterwards.

Eventually the ninety minutes were up. Only injury time.

The tension in the ground was hard to bear. The noise of the crowd less intense. Sudden pauses before a group of fans would try to start a chant going.

The Russian fans were booing. They could see their dream of going to the World Cup disappearing.

The England fans, on the other hand, were jubilant. A draw was enough. If the score stayed this way it meant England would very possibly be going to the finals. At Russia's expense.

Then Danny noticed something: a group of four

men coming around the edge of the pitch. Dressed in black, head to foot. He couldn't make out any of them, to see if he recognized their faces. But he was worried. Very worried. His whole trip had been dogged by these sinister men. Tupolev's men, there was no question.

The fourth official put his board up: three minutes of injury time.

The Russians took heart from this, upping their game. They were playing the long ball now. No neat passing through midfield any more. Now it was: get the ball, hoof it into the penalty area, head it down to a striker.

But the England centre backs would just head it away. There was no joy for Russia. The ball just wouldn't come down for one of their players to control it.

Until the last minute. The last attack.

Another Russian missile came flying into the box from the halfway line. The giant striker leapt and headed it back across the penalty area. Right to a small Russian who'd only just come on to the pitch.

He pulled his leg back and volleyed the ball towards the bottom right corner of the net.

McGee was wrong-footed when the ball hit an English defender, ricocheting instead to the bottom left corner of the net. He could only watch and shift his feet as it rolled towards the line.

And then he dived.

Dived the length of the goal.

It was impossible that a man could change the direction of his body like that; but McGee was doing it.

His large hand closed over the ball as two Russian players lunged at it, kicking McGee hard in the back.

But McGee had his body curled up, the ball close to his chest.

As he stood to release the ball, the whole stadium applauded his save – including the Russians.

Danny noticed the four men in black had stopped at the back of McGee's goal. He saw McGee glance back at them, just as the referee put the whistle to his lips and blew.

That was it.

Full time.

A massive cheer. From the England fans.

Then Danny noticed that McGee was trying to signal to the bench. But the England players mobbed him. He'd saved the game. England were one step closer to going to the World Cup finals.

And then, to everyone's shock, the floodlights – and every light in the stadium – went out.

Nobody could see a thing.

## THE ABDUCTION

Danny knew immediately that something was very wrong.

The game over.

The lights out.

The men in black.

He called out to Holt. But Holt must have gone back inside to file his match report. So Danny acted. He couldn't stop himself. McGee had got *him* out of trouble; now he wanted to reciprocate.

He ran to the foot of the stand. There was just enough light to see the steps and the pitch. But not across it.

He vaulted the advertisement hoardings – and was on the pitch. He could see the players just standing there. Unsure if the game had ended or not.

But not McGee. McGee had disappeared.

Danny ran to the goal mouth. He could make out no lights except from under the stands. Emergency lighting. And there – silhouettes against the only light in the stadium – he saw a scrum of people, close together, struggling towards the exit.

He set off after them. They had McGee. Danny knew it.

He ran at medium speed. He didn't want to be exhausted when he reached them. And he knew they were moving slowly. Slower than him.

Danny heard the English fans chanting as he dived under the stadium into the plastic tunnel where the players had emerged for each half of the match.

Now that he knew McGee was straight, he wanted to do everything he could to rescue him. He had doubted him, thought he was going to throw the game. And he felt guilty.

He heard voices. McGee calling.

'Help! Someone! They're going to –'

Then McGee's voice was muffled.

Under the stands, a strip of emergency lights ran along the ceiling. Danny spotted McGee being led away; but now he looked as if he was happy to be going.

*A gun*, Danny thought. *They must have a gun on him.*

What on earth could he do? Where would they take McGee? What would they do with him?

There were other people under the stand. Dozens of Russia fans, some with children, leaving in disgust immediately after the final whistle and the darkness. Even though it was dangerously dark to leave.

Danny followed McGee and his abductors. But not too close. He wanted surprise on his side. That was his one advantage.

Then he had an idea. From a book again. One he'd read to his dad. Cause a distraction. Shout something to change everybody's behaviour. Create a stampede. Or at least a blockage.

He shouted, '*Avtograf!*' Then again: '*Avtograf!*'

Several people – especially those with children – looked at him.

Danny waved his arm. And jogged towards McGee and his abductors, holding out his notebook and a pencil.

'*Avtograf!*' he shouted again.

And it worked. Several children were following him. He felt like the Pied Piper of Hamelin.

'*Avtograf!*' he shouted once more.

McGee and the four men in black were suddenly surrounded by fans, mostly children, holding scraps of paper and pens out to McGee. Even though this man had probably stopped their team from qualifying for the World Cup, they wanted to meet him. He was an English Premier League player: one of the elite of footballers.

Danny watched as McGee began signing autographs, while trying to push away from his captors.

All the men in black could do was try to keep as close to him as possible. There was no way out for them.

Danny smiled. Now he needed to catch McGee's eye.

He'd stopped his abduction.

*Now* he needed to abduct McGee from his abductors.

## *WE MEET AGAIN*

Danny hadn't looked behind him since the autograph scrum had started. He'd not seen the man standing there. The man thinking about what *he* should do next.

'Danny,' the man said in a soft voice. So soft – and English – that Danny assumed it was Holt.

Danny turned round, about to ask what they could do.

To be faced by Sir Richard Gawthorpe.

His nemesis looked calm. Not angry. Or frustrated. Or scared, even.

'We meet again,' Sir Richard said.

Danny jumped. Literally. Like a shot of electricity had gone through him. He had to pull himself together. Not lose control. Not let Sir Richard see how scared he was.

'It's over,' Danny said.

'Is it?'

'Yes. I've got –' Danny went for his pocket.

'Danny,' Sir Richard smiled, glancing at the wall beside to him. 'It's not over. Even if you get out of here alive, no one will believe whatever story you have cobbled together. This is Russia. Things work differently here, Danny.'

Danny was about to speak when he saw Sir Richard's face light up. And then suddenly the man was shouting. At the top of his voice. 'FIRE! FIRE! FIRE!'

Danny was so surprised he stumbled.

Sir Richard pushed in a fire alarm on the wall next to him. The noise was dramatic. First the ringing. Then the sound of hundreds of feet running and hundreds of voices crying out.

The mood changed immediately. Parents picked up sons and daughters from the scrum and ran. Fire doors burst open.

Danny turned to see McGee being grabbed again and dragged away, through a fire door to a waiting black people-carrier.

Then he felt his legs go from under him. And a punch to his back. And Sir Richard was standing over him.

'If I had time . . . I'd kill you,' Sir Richard said. 'If I meet you again I *will* kill you.'

Then Sir Richard was off, heading for the black vehicle.

Danny staggered to his feet. This was his last chance.

As he ran, he saw that the road was open for the people-carrier – fenced off from the fans. It would be out of there in seconds.

So he ran faster. Ran like he'd never run before. He had to try and save Matt McGee. If he could just make it to the car.

In seconds he was almost level with Sir Richard.

Sir Richard dived into the car, to avoid what he thought would be Danny attacking him.

But Danny had other thoughts. He was going for the *front* of the car.

He heard the engine rev as the car door slammed shut behind Sir Richard. And Danny waited in front of it, holding his mobile phone out in front of him.

Danny stood there, convinced he was about to disappear under a large heavy vehicle – and to die in a very painful way.

The car lunged at him. Then braked. Like an animal snapping, then retracting. But not biting.

Now Danny could only hear the engine idling and his own heart hammering. Then a door opening.

Sir Richard came from the back of the car.

'What?'

Danny could feel his hand shaking violently, still holding the phone. He could barely control his emotions. He'd switched his phone to video and began to record.

'WHAT?' Sir Richard shouted.

'I sent a film. From the reception,' Danny said. 'Tupolev talking to Matt McGee about their deal. I sent it to England.'

Danny saw Sir Richard's eyes narrow.

'And I have a film of you on the steps when McGee attacked Skatie. With Tupolev's men behind you.' Danny watched for another physical reaction. But there was nothing. 'And I'm filming you now. But *this* is the only clear film of you I have. The one on the steps: you can't really see it's you. But this. This *does* show it's you. I can give you this. Now.'

Danny saw Sir Richard's shoulders drop.

'Let McGee go,' Danny said, his voice trembling. 'And you can have it.'

Sir Richard looked confused. Like he was doing something he didn't want to do.

'Let him go and I'll move out of the way,' Danny said. 'No dead boy. No abducted footballer. No film of you. Just a film of Tupolev.'

Sir Richard shook his head, looking at the ground.

Then, behind them, the lights came on. A massive flood of light. So bright everyone was blinded briefly.

They heard the noise of tens of thousands of fans leaving their seats in the stadium. Headed their way. About to block the roads and the paths for hours.

Sir Richard gestured to the car, pointing at McGee, then outside.

At first the men in the car refused to act. Then Sir Richard pulled his own phone out of his pocket. He pointed at it. Mouthed 'Dmitri' at the driver.

The rest happened quickly.

McGee emerged from the car and ran back into the stadium.

Danny threw his phone to Sir Richard.

Sir Richard got in the car. But before he did, he turned to Danny. 'You're lucky I have more important concerns right now. I meant what I said in there,' he said. 'If I see you again, I will kill you.'

Danny shrugged. He wanted to say something witty, but decided to leave Sir Richard with a silence. Sometimes silence said more than words.

'And when I do,' Sir Richard went on, 'I'll be back in charge of City. That's a promise.'

Danny shook his head and smiled. 'Never,' he said.

And with that the black people-carrier was gone.

# THURSDAY

## *PRESENTS*

Moscow Domodedovo Airport felt good. Once Danny was airside and mingling with hundreds of other England fans.

It was safe to be in numbers. He hoped.

Danny wanted to go home. Home to his dad's cooking, his mum's rushing off to work, his sister's jibes.

He enjoyed travelling, but he'd had enough for a while.

Once they had got through security, Holt had gone to sit down with a plate of chips and his laptop. He had some changes to make to his article, he said.

So Danny decided to go and spend his roubles. He still had most of the £100 he'd got from the Post Office.

He bought his mum a mug with Vladimir Putin, the former – or present, he wasn't sure – leader of Russia on it. His mum liked mugs. When you poured hot water into it Putin's stern expression broke out into a chilling smile. He thought his mum would like that.

For his dad he bought a thriller: *Gorky Park*. Based

in Moscow. They'd watched the film together on TV; now they could read the book. That was a Moscow adventure story Danny *could* tell his dad about.

He bought Paul a Russian football T-shirt. Paul liked foreign team tops. And now England had put one over on Russia he'd be able to wear it without feeling like a traitor.

But what should he buy for Charlotte?

Something you'd buy for a friend? Another T-shirt? Or something else?

Danny watched other men in the duty-free shop. What were they buying? They'd be getting presents for their wives and girlfriends. He could see what they chose. Not that Charlotte was his girlfriend. But she was his friend. And a girl. Danny felt confused.

Perfume. Chocolates. A bag. A scarf. An ornament. That's what men were buying. There was so much choice. But Danny didn't have a clue what was the right thing for him to get.

He wished his sister was here. She would tell him what was nice. She was good – if not at some things – at least at buying presents.

Danny plumped for a gold chain in the end. Just a small chain. Like the one she'd had until a few months ago, but it had broken. A fine chain, not a heavy one.

He felt shy buying it. What was he *doing*? And the

woman at the counter reeked so much of perfume, Danny felt slightly faint.

Danny had around £20 left for himself.

What could he get?

A book? A Russia T-shirt? A small model of St Basil's Cathedral? Yes. He'd like that. It was a building – and a night – he'd never forget.

And then he saw a set of Russian dolls. Six over-painted wooden dolls that fitted inside each other. That's what Emily had asked him for, the day he felt like killing her.

Danny grinned. He didn't really need anything. He had memories.

So he bought the Russian dolls for his sister.

In a suite of the Cosmonaut Hotel, not so far from the airport, another drama was unfolding.

Dmitri Tupolev was sitting in a chair examining Sir Richard Gawthorpe. The Englishman was sitting on the floor, his hands tied behind his back.

No one else was in the room.

'You have gone against me,' the Russian said.

'No. I saved you,' Sir Richard replied in a calm voice. He was not going to be cowed by the man who had become his adversary.

The Russian shrugged. 'You no longer exist, Sir Richard.'

Now it was the Englishman's turn to shrug.

And then the ground shook and the walls began to move.

# *FRIDAY*

## *EXCLUSIVE*

Mid-morning on Friday, Danny went to the newsagent's to get the paper. The first edition of the *Evening Post*. Holt had called the night before to say his piece was in the next day.

### RUSSIAN TRIED TO FIX ENGLAND QUALIFIER – EXCLUSIVE

#### THE *EVENING POST* TALKS TO ENGLAND HERO, MATT MCGEE

After the heroics of Wednesday night, when the England keeper almost single-handedly kept England in the running for World Cup qualification, I met up with the enigma that is Matt McGee.

And he told me a story that is quite literally unbelievable. Unbelievable, that is, until you hear the news coming out of Russia this weekend.

'First, I want to set the record straight about the counterfeit money,' McGee told me. 'I did have the money on me. I had it because a friend of mine gave it to me. He owed me some cash. But I didn't know it was counterfeit. I was convicted because I refused to give up the name of that person. I did that for my own reasons. I have paid my penalty. That's the end of that for me.'

But then Matt McGee launched into the story that will echo through the stands at football stadiums across the world for weeks to come. It comes after he disappeared at the end of England's qualifier in Russia – only to emerge from the crowds minutes later.

'They tried to fix the game,' he said. 'First they offered to pay me. To wipe out my debts. Then they threatened me. With death.'

McGee took a pause at this point in the interview to have a sip of water. But he soon regained his composure.

'A group of Russians got to me and threatened me. One of them was the well-known oligarch Dmitri Tupolev. He asked me to fumble a corner and give away a penalty.'

And did the England player say no?

'I didn't say no,' McGee said. 'I was afraid for my life. This guy is famous for killing people. I just didn't say yes.'

I tried to get more details out of McGee, but he declined. He has just signed a two-million-pound contract for the story of his blackmail and abduction with the independent publisher Frank Books who hope to have it out in time for Christmas.

When I tried to push him further, asking if selling his story to a publisher was in the public interest, he was upset. 'I did what was in the public interest by not throwing the game, by helping England qualify for the World Cup. As you know,' he went on, 'I am in financial meltdown and need some money. The book deal has saved me. And now I hope to live a better life.'

I asked him what he'd do with the two million.

He was candid with his reply. 'It'll go two ways. A million to write off my debts. A million to a charity that helps survivors of the Chernobyl nuclear power disaster in Russia.'

Next I asked Matt about rumours that he was involved in the attack on Robert Skatie, the man who was meant to play in Russia on Wednesday.

'I attacked him so that he'd not be able to play,' McGee said. 'I knew that they would come for him next as he had been picked to play the game. They came to me because they assumed I'd be playing. But I also knew that Robert would have been under much more pressure than me. He has a young family; I have none. What if they had threatened his wife and two small children?'

News coming from the FA confirms that Robert

Skatie is fine after his Moscow fall. As is Alex Finn, who had a car accident in the UK days before the game.

'Alex had been got to as well,' McGee said. 'They threatened him before the home game a week and a half ago. But he ignored them. He played so well in the home game. The crash was set up. By Tupolev and his English partner.'

The *Evening Post* knows the identity of the Englishman in question. But it needs more time to research the facts before it prints the full story tomorrow.

Danny smiled as he read the story. Once again he'd not even got a mention.

And that was how he wanted it.

He'd had a private thank-you from Matt McGee. A phone call. And a promise that he would not be mentioned in the autobiography.

That was enough for Danny.

The only thing he wasn't sure about was what Anton would write about Sir Richard tomorrow.

If he'd reveal who he was. If his boss would let him.

Whatever he did write, Danny knew that if he was going to be a real Football Detective, his next case would be his biggest. Making sure that Sir Richard Gawthorpe

– or whatever he called himself now – did not get control of his beloved City football club.

And he knew it was a case he'd have to open soon.

Had Danny turned on a TV at that moment, he'd have seen breaking news.

A hotel had blown up in Moscow. Eighty people were dead. The Russian government reported that they had arrested a group of Chechen separatists believed to have been responsible.

One notable person was dead. The target of the attack. Dmitri Tupolev, member of the Russian parliament and oligarch. Along with his unknown visitor.

## ACKNOWLEDGEMENTS

As always, first thanks go to Rebecca and Iris. For everything. This book is for you.

Big thanks too to David Luxton, my agent, who is a great guide and friend. Thank you.

I travelled to Moscow twice to research this book and need to thank Igor Goldes, Julia, Jonathan Wilson and Evgeny Kuzmin for their help. Also the Russian government's Department of Mass Communication and Media, and Academia Rossica.

People in Russia were very warm and welcoming on both my trips. I didn't meet anyone as nasty as Dmitri Tupolev. Fortunately.

Dan Jones was my guide on my first trip to Moscow. He was a great help. Thank you, Dan.

I try to make my books as accurate as I can so that they sound like they are about real football in the UK. Thank you to Ollie Holt, Richard Whitehead and Matt Wilkinson.

I'd like to thank everyone at Puffin for their inspired and hard work.

Thank you to the other two members of my writing

group, Sophie Hannah and James Nash. Also, thanks to Daniel Taylor (Birmingham City) for reading the first draft and giving me great feedback. And to Nikki for reading the book too.

# Ten things you (possibly) didn't know about TOM PALMER

Tom was possibly left as newborn in a box at the door of an adoption home in 1967.

**He has got an adopted dad and a step-dad, but has never met his real dad.**

Tom's best job – before being an author – was a milkman. He delivered milk for nine years.

**He once scored two goals direct from the corner flag in the same game. It was very windy.**

Tom did not read a book by himself until he was seventeen.

**In 1990 Tom wrecked his knee while playing for Bulmershe College in Reading. He didn't warm up and has regretted it ever since.**

He was the UK's 1997 Bookseller of the Year.

**He met his wife in the Sahara Desert.**

Tom has been to watch over 500 Leeds United games, with Leeds winning 307. He once went for twenty-one years without missing a home game. His wife has been ten times, with Leeds winning every time.

**Tom once met George Best in a London pub. Tom wanted to borrow his newspaper to find out the football scores. George kindly obliged.**